Amy Cross is the author of more than 100 horror, paranormal, fantasy and thriller novels.

OTHER TITLES
BY AMY CROSS INCLUDE

*American Coven*
*Annie's Room*
*The Ash House*
*Asylum*
*B&B*
*Better the Devil*
*The Bride of Ashbyrn House*
*The Camera Man*
*The Curse of Wetherley House*
*The Devil, the Witch and the Whore*
*Devil's Briar*
*The Dog*
*Eli's Town*
*The Farm*
*The Ghost of Molly Holt*
*The Ghosts of Lakeforth Hotel*
*The Girl Who Never Came Back*
*Haunted*
*The Haunting of Blackwych Grange*
*The Haunting of Marshall Heights*
*Like Stones on a Crow's Back*
*The Night Girl*
*Perfect Little Monsters & Other Stories*
*Stephen*
*The Shades*
*The Soul Auction*
*Tenderling*
*Ward Z*

# *Days 1 to 4*

AMY CROSS

First published by Dark Season Books,
United Kingdom, 2018



First published in April 2013 as part of *Mass Extinction Event: The Complete First* Series. This edition originally published in July 2018



ISBN: 9781717962720

Also available in e-book format.

www.amycross.com

# CONTENTS

# DAYS 1 TO 4

# PROLOGUE

*Three weeks ago*

IT STARTS WITH A man in a crowd at an airport. The kind of man no-one ever notices.

But he's used to not being noticed.

Shuffling through the sea of bodies, the man keeps his hands in the pockets of his light beige jacket. His fingers are wrapped around a pair of glass vials, each of which is airtight. The vials are just a couple of inches long and half an inch wide, but their contents have the potential to spread around the world many, many times over. It's almost as if the man has two entirely new worlds in his pockets, ready to release them at a moment's notice. He's been waiting for this moment for so long, and now it's finally here.

Most importantly, the glass of these vials is particularly thin; so thin, in fact, that even the slightest pressure could cause them to break.

The man hates people. He detests every other human being on the planet. That's why he created the virus in these vials, and it's why he's holding them so tight. As he's bumped and knocked by people in the crowd, he knows that at any moment one of these rude assholes is going to thump rudely into him and cause his fingers to break the glass of the vial. It seems somewhat poetic to have things happen like this, and the man can't help smiling as he continues to make his way through the check-in area. He's not here to catch a plane, though; he's just here to experience the rudeness and lack of thought of his fellow man.

"Out of the way!" shouts a businessman, charging through the crowd as he races to catch his flight. He slams into the man, who gasps at the thought that finally the vials might break. But they don't. Somehow, miraculously, the vials remain intact. The businessman merely scuttles off into the distance, leaving the man to watch him go. That was exactly the kind of rude, inconsiderate asshole who the man hoped would break the vials, but it doesn't matter. The world, the man reminds himself, is full of assholes. There'll be another one along any -

"Oh, I'm sorry!" says a woman, bumping

into the man and shattering one of the vials in the man's pocket.

The man turns to find a blonde, middle-aged woman carrying a toddler in her arms.

"I'm so sorry," she continues. "I hope I didn't hurt you".

The man stares at her for a moment. This isn't quite how he expected it to happen, but it's too late to change things now. Besides, all that matters is that the first vial is broken. In his other pocket, he squeezes his fingers together and the second vial breaks.

"It's quite alright," he says, his heart pounding at the thought that all his work has finally paid off. "Please don't give it a second thought".

"Sorry," the woman mutters again, before pushing past him.

"Excuse me," the man says. "Can I ask... What's your name?"

The woman turns back to look at him. "Karen," she says, before pausing. "Why?"

"No reason," the man replies, pausing for a moment. "My name's Joseph," he says eventually.

The woman smiles politely. "Okay. Well, sorry again, Joseph". With that, she turns and hurries into the crowd, disappearing from view within seconds.

Taking a deep breath, Joseph stands and imagines the contents of the vial spreading through the airport. Carried in the lungs of everyone in the building, carried onto planes, carried through the air to other cities, and remaining dormant all the time until finally the right moment will arrive and people will start to die. The virus has been very precisely engineered so that it won't be noticed until it has spread all over the world. Smiling, Joseph turns and starts heading for the exit. He figures he might as well go and have one final drink at his favorite bar, and reflect upon the fact that the secret to immortality has turned out to be so simple: kill as many other people as possible.

# DAY 1

# ELIZABETH

*Manhattan*

"HANG ON!" I say, tucking the phone under my chin as I carry the bottles of cola over to the sink. "Henry!" I shout at the top of my voice, hoping against hope that my brother will be able to hear me over the din of the laptop in the next room. He's watching some kind of cartoon, with the volume turned up to full. "Henry! Can you come through here for a minute?" I wait for him to reply. "Henry?"

"What's going on there?" my mother asks over the phone. "It sounds like absolute chaos".

"It's not *chaos*," I say, putting the bottles down and then sliding the kitchen drawer out to search for an opener. "It's cool, Mom. It's just that everything's happening all at once and... It doesn't matter. Did you have a good birthday?"

"Oh, delightful," my mother replies drolly, her voice dripping with sarcasm. "A whole night alone with your father. Wining, dining and whining. What could be more enjoyable?"

"That's nice," I mutter. "Listen, I wanted to say that I'm -"

"I swear," he continues, interrupting me, "your father goes out of his way to cause embarrassing scenes when we're out. Do you know how many times he sent his main course back to the kitchen?"

"I'm sure it was lots of times," I reply, "but listen, Mom, I just wanted to tell you that I'm -"

"Next time, he can cook his own fucking steak".

"Mom, I'm -"

"You should have seen the look on the waiter's face. *So* embarrassing, Elizabeth. I could have curled up and died right there and then".

I sigh. "But you had a good time, right?"

"Hmph!"

"Listen, Mom," I say after a moment, "I wanted to talk about what I said the other night, before you left. I didn't mean it. I'm -"

"Oh, Elizabeth, do we have to go over this now?" she asks, putting on her most tired-sounding voice. "We'll talk about it when we get back, okay?"

"Yeah," I continue, "but I just wanted to say that I'm -"

"We'll be home around *three*," she says firmly, as if to emphasize the fact that she really doesn't want this conversation to continue. "Do you think you can manage to keep things ticking over at home until then, Elizabeth?"

"Of course," I reply, searching through the kitchen drawer. "Where's the bottle opener?"

"Use the one on the wall," she snaps back at me.

Grabbing one of the bottles, I head over to the electric opener next to the fridge. I hate using the electrical appliances when we have perfectly good non-electric ones that people just keep misplacing. It's a total waste of energy. Then again, my parents have the time and the money to buy every labor-saving device on the planet, which means our entire apartment is filled, wall to wall and floor to ceiling, with an array of devices that only seem to *add* to our stress levels. Convenience has never seemed so inconvenient.

"This airport is a fucking nightmare," she continues. "I don't know what's going on, but people are just so rude these days. I've almost been knocked over four times, and all I'm trying to do is claim my fucking baggage. You'd think people would be a little more considerate of one another's needs, but apparently not. Welcome to the modern world, where nobody gives a crap anymore".

"Henry!" I shout. "Can you get your ass through here?" I wait for a reply, but all I hear is the sound of his laptop. My brother is taking full advantage of our parents' absence, and he's spent all morning watching cartoons. He knows full well that I don't have the ability to force him to do anything, so he's going to go on his stupid little power trip and ignore every request I make of him. To top it all off, when our parents get home, he's the one who'll get treated like an angel, while I'll be told to tidy up. At his age, though, he should know better. "Henry!" I shout again.

"Don't yell at him," my mother says. "Yelling doesn't work with Henry. Do you know what works?"

"Years and years of consistently good parenting?" I mutter darkly.

"Don't try to be smart with me, Elizabeth".

"I wasn't *trying* to be smart," I say, hitting the button on the electric opener. For a second, it starts up, before suddenly the power fails completely. The lights turn off, the hum of the air-conditioning winds down, and the laptop goes silent as the router dies. "Huh," I say, looking across the gloomy apartment. "There's no power".

"What do you mean?" my mother barks.

"Elizabeth!" Henry screams from the front room. "Why's everything gone off? What did you do?"

"There's no electricity," I tell my mother again as I flick the bottle opener on and off several times. The whole apartment is kind of gloomy. "Where's the fuse box?"
"The *what*?"
"The fuse box," I say, walking through to the hallway. "We must have blown a fuse or something. Where's the box?"

"I have no idea what you're talking about," she replies haughtily, "and please watch your tone when you're speaking to me".

"I didn't swear!"

"I don't know where the *fuse box* is," she continues, stressing those two words as if they're completely alien to her, "and I doubt your father does, either. I don't think we even have one. Why would we? This is the twenty-first century, Elizabeth. People like us don't have fuse boxes, for God's sake. There's probably just one big fuse box for the whole building, so Giedo's undoubtedly heading down there to fix it as we speak. I'm sure you'll have power in a couple of seconds".

Sighing, I head through to the front room.

"Why's there no power?" Henry asks, staring at me as if I'm personally responsible for this latest fuck-up. He's sitting cross-legged in front of the laptop, leaning back on the side of the sofa. He's only sixteen years old, but Henry's already cultivated a very grand and very solid impression of his own importance. From the scowl on his face, you'd think the whole of New York had conspired to have a power cut solely to piss him off.

"There's a blackout," I tell him.

"Duh!" he replies. "I know that. *Why's* there a blackout, and how long's it gonna last?"

"I have no idea," I say.

"Tell him it'll just be a few minutes," my mother barks from the other end of the phone.

"You don't know that," I hiss back at her.

"Elizabeth," she says, "power cuts are very rare, and when they happen, they're fixed quickly. They have little people to work on these things".

"Who are 'they' and what 'little people' do they have?" I ask, marveling at my mother's understanding of how the world works.

"Jesus Christ, this isn't a third-world country," she sighs. "Tell your brother that everything's going to be okay. *Okay*?"

"It's okay, Henry," I say reluctantly. "Everything's going to be okay".

"Tell him Giedo's fixing it," my mother adds.

"Giedo's fixing it," I say with a sigh. "Probably," I mutter under my breath, as I turn and head back through to the kitchen. Something about this day just feels a little 'off' and I can't wait for it to be over. I hate it when my parents go away and leave me in charge; my brother's a spoiled little brat and I don't see why I should have to babysit him when all he's gonna do is sit around making demands and treating me like a piece of crap. "Is Dad there?" I ask. "Can I talk to Dad?"

"He's still in the bathroom," she replies. I stand and listen to the sound of pushing and shoving. There are some raised voices, and finally I hear my mother let out a loud sigh.

"Well, that's just wonderful!" she continues eventually. "Do you what just happened? Half a dozen men in military get-up just came running through the baggage reclaim room as if the whole world was on fire. They were carrying great big guns, slung over their shoulders and swinging about so much, they almost hit several people in the eye. It's as if they don't care about the people in their path. I can't believe what the world is coming to, Elizabeth. There's clearly no respect for anyone".

"I guess not," I say, flicking the light switch on and off a few times, with no luck. "It's a miracle no-one got hurt," she adds. "They just came storming through here as if they own the place. Jesus Christ, you put a uniform on a man, Elizabeth, and he thinks he can do whatever he wants. If they -" Suddenly there's a brief click, followed by silence.

I wait for her to continue.

"If they what?" I ask.

Silence.

"Mom?" I say after a moment. "If they what?" I wait a few seconds, before I realize that I can't hear anything at all through the speaker. The line's gone completely dead. "Great," I say, putting the phone down and walking back over to the kitchen counter. It seems like this is one of those days where everything starts going wrong. I take the cola bottle from the opener and place it on the counter, before grabbing a small knife from nearby and using it to carefully slip the bottle cap away. Once that's done, I grab the other bottle and do the same; this time, however, there's a little more pressure holding the cap in place, and the knife slips out of the groove. The bottle falls over as the blade slices into my thumb just below the nail. Shocked, I pull the knife away and throw it to the ground.

"Fuck!" I shout, standing back and watching as the bottle rolls off the counter and smashes against the floor. "Fuck!" I shout again.

"Well done!" Henry calls through to me. "That was your bottle, not mine. You know that, right? I'm not having the broken one!"

"Fuck!" I say again, looking down at my thumb and seeing that I've cut a fair-sized gash straight through one side. Bright red blood is already starting to run down onto my hand, so I hurry over to the sink and turn the tap on. Sticking my thumb where I expect the water to come out, I wait for several seconds before trying the tap again. Nothing. I turn the handle all the way to the other side, but all that comes out is a brief, thin dribble that soon dries up. Meanwhile, my thumb is continuing to bleed heavily.

"Can you bring my bottle through?" Henry shouts. "Can you do it now? I'm literally dying of thirst in here!"

Ignoring him, I examine the wound on the tip of my thumb and see that it's quite deep. I must have gone almost through to the bone. Taking a deep breath, I force myself to remember that there's no reason to panic. No-one ever died of a cut thumb. Not in Manhattan, anyway.

"Elizabeth!" Henry calls out, sounding increasingly impatient.

"In a minute!" I call back to him, grabbing a piece of paper towel and wrapping it around the thumb. As I turn to carry the cola bottle through to my brother, I glance over at the window and see something unusual outside. I walk over and stare out at the Manhattan skyline, and finally I realize what's wrong: there's no power anywhere. All the buildings are dulled against the bright afternoon sky, and looking down at the street I can see cars stuck at the nearest intersection as they try to negotiate the crossing without any traffic signals. It's as if all the electricity in the entire city has suddenly been switched off, and a blanket of calm has descended as far as the eye can see.

# THOMAS

*Oklahoma*

COMING UP AROUND the back of the barn, I stop dead in my tracks as soon as I see Joe's truck parked out front of the house. It's been a while since Joe was last allowed to head into town on his own, but it looks like maybe he's been given the keys back at last. That's good. Having Joe confined to the farm was unnatural; Joe's the kind of guy who needs to be able to stretch his legs, and it wasn't fair of our parents to clip his wings just because of one small vehicular mishap. Besides, I miss going driving with Joe; it used to be just about the only fun thing to do around here.

"You just go straight there and back," our father says as he comes out of the house, limping slightly on his bad leg. He glances back at Joe's, who's just a few steps behind. "You don't go anywhere else. You don't take any detours. You got that? Just town and the gas station, and stick to a sensible speed. I've only this morning finished banging the panels back into shape after your last excursion, and it's not an experience I want to repeat. And don't forget to fill the tank back up before you come home. I don't want an empty truck sitting in the driveway, okay? There's other people besides you who need to use this truck".

Without saying a word, Joe throws his backpack into the rear of the truck, before heading around to the driver's side door.

"I asked if you understood what I just said," our father continues.

"I speak English, don't I?" Joe says, climbing into the truck and pulling the door shut. "I went to school every day like a good boy, so I know what all those fancy words mean". That's typical of Joe: he's always pretty sarcastic, especially when he's talking to our father. Deep down, though, Joe's a good person: he's got a heart of gold buried beneath that rough exterior. Other people maybe don't see it like that, but they don't know him well enough; he's my brother, though, so I can see right through him. He's cool. One day, I'm gonna be just like him.

"It's not only -" our father starts to say, but

Joe starts the engine, floors the throttle and accelerates out of the driveway. "Hey, wait a minute!" our father calls after him, but it's obviously too late. He's left standing in the yard, watching as Joe heads off into the distance.

Realizing that this might be my best chance to hang out with Joe for a while, I turn and race across the field. I can see the truck following the curve of the road as Joe heads to the junction, and I'm pretty sure I've got a chance of catching up to him. Racing across the uneven ground, I see Joe indicating to turn left, and finally he pulls onto the main road. I leap over the fence and make my way through the mud bank before running out into the middle of the road just in time to make Joe slow down.

"What do you want?" he asks, sounding as if he's irritated.

"Where are you going?" I reply.

"Town".

"How come?"

"The old bastard needs something. Or wants something. Or just fancies getting his hands on something. I don't know. Some kind of wire. You know how it is. He gets some stupid idea in his head, and I'm the one who has to go running off to fetch a bunch of junk".

"And he's letting you drive again?"

"Why wouldn't he?"

"Can I come?" I ask, shielding my eyes from the sun.

"Why the hell would you want to come?" he asks. "I'm only going to Scottsville".

"I've got nothing else to do," I tell him. "Power's off, so I can't watch TV, and I can't play any games if the internet's down. If I hang around here, Dad'll eventually find me and give me some stupid job. I'd rather be heading off to Scottsville with you".

Joe stares at me for a moment. "Read a book," he says eventually. He puts the truck in gear, ready to drive away, but I run around to the other side, pull the door open, and climb inside. "What the fuck are you doing, Thomas?" Joe asks, staring at me as if I'm some kind of madman.

"I'm coming with you," I tell him.

He sighs. "No, you're not".

"It'll be fun!" I say. "Come on... please? There's a power cut, so it's not like I've got anything else to do. Anyway, it's way cooler hanging out with you than sitting around at home".

"You think I'm cool?" He laughs. "You really need to get out of the house more, kid".

Sighing, he puts the truck in gear and eases us away down the road. He hasn't said anything, but I know that this is his way of acquiescing to my demand. I knew I could talk him around; after all, despite his constant protestations to the contrary,

Joe and I are very similar. People often comment on how we look quite alike, even though he's almost ten years older than me, and we certainly have very similar characters. We're both stubborn and independent, and we're both prone to attracting trouble occasionally. There are differences, though; I don't have moments of madness where I do completely stupid things, but other than that I reckon Joe and I make the perfect team.

"So you're talking to Dad again," I say eventually as we head along the road. I can't help noticing that Joe's driving pretty fast, but I figure there's no point saying anything; he'd probably speed up, just to make a point.

"Am I?" he asks.

"I saw you".

"There's different kind of talking," he says, keeping his eyes on the road.

"He let you take the truck out". "He had no choice. His hernia's playing up again. He knows he can't drive".

"But it's a big deal for him to -"

"Drop it".

"Why?"

"Because I said so".

"Sorry".

We drive on in silence. I want to tell Joe that I'm glad he's finally talking to our father, but I know what my brother's like: he'd probably kick me out of the truck and make me walk home. That's the problem with Joe; you can't be completely honest with him, because he tends to take honest sentiments and twist them around until they seem dark and bitter. Still, I know that he and our father are getting closer again. Maybe they'll never be best friends, but they can handle being around one another. That's progress, at least. It means that maybe, when our father eventually wants to retire, Joe might reconsider his refusal to take over the running of the farm.

"So what wires are we getting?" I ask eventually.

"No idea," Joe replies. "He wrote it down. I'm just gonna hand the piece of paper over to old Steve and let him sort it out. At least that way, there's not much chance of me ending up with the wrong stuff".

"Yeah," I say, turning to him, "and you're like a -" Suddenly I spot something in the distance; up ahead of us, parked slightly off the road, there's a police patrol car. It's far from unusual to find one of the local cops snoozing in his vehicle during the mornings, but something looks wrong this time; the car's tilted slightly into a ditch that runs by the side of the road, and the driver's side door is open.

"Fucking cops," Joe says, slowing the truck as we drive past the patrol car.

"Do you think he's okay?" I ask, staring

through the window and seeing that the vehicle seems empty.

"Fucking hope not," Joe replies.

"Yeah, but -" At that moment, I see movement on the seat of the police car, as if someone's slumped over on the seat. "Hey, stop the truck!" I yell at Joe.

"No way".

"I think he's hurt".

"So what?"

"So stop the truck!"

To my surprise, Joe slams his foot on the brakes and we screech to a halt. "You go check on him," Joe tells me after a moment. "If he's dying, let me know so I can go piss on his face".

Realizing that it's pointless to argue, I get out of the truck and walk toward the patrol car. Joe's never been a big fan of the local police, mainly because they've picked him up so many times for being drunk. It's not as if I'm fond of the cops either, but at least I'm curious to see if this guy's okay. Cop or no cop, he's still a human being. As I approach the car, I can hear a vague scrabbling sound from inside, and I walk slowly around the side until I can see into the front seat.

And there he is.

One cop, slumped over with his face pressed against the seat. I don't know what's wrong with him, but my first thought is that maybe he's had a heart attack or something. He seems to be clutching his belly as if he's in pain.

"You okay?" I ask.

He doesn't reply. It's almost as if he hasn't even heard me.

"Hey," I say after a moment. "Are you okay?"

Still no reply.

"It's okay," I tell him. "We're gonna get help". Turning to the truck, I wave in an attempt to get Joe's attention. "Hey!" I shout eventually. "Joe, seriously! Come here! I think he's hurt!"

"How bad?" Joe shouts back at me.

"I don't know. I think -" At that moment, the cop seems to react to our voices: he shifts position slightly, and finally he looks up at me. I'm instantly shocked by the state of his face: he looks so thin and ill, and his skin's a kind of pale yellow and gray color. Although his eyes are staring straight at me, it's almost as if he's not really able to process the fact that I'm here. He sure doesn't say anything, and he breathing seems labored and raspy. Whatever's wrong with him, he's deathly sick and he needs help fast.

"Come on!" Joe shouts. "We're running late! I ain't helping no cop".

"Come and look!" I shout back. "Seriously, I think something's really wrong with him! I'm not joking!"

After a moment, Joe gets out of the truck and slams the door shut before stomping over to join me. He's clearly not happy about being disturbed, although a smile spreads on his face as soon as he sees the emaciated figure of the cop. "Well," he says, "what we got here? You weren't kidding when you said he was sick, were you?"

"What's wrong with him?" I ask.

"He's a cop. They all get like this eventually. Something to do with selling their soul to the Devil".

"Seriously, Joe".

He shrugs. "I don't know. Maybe he's got some kind of STD on his face from hanging out with too many whores".

"We've gotta help him," I say.

"You wanna put him out of his misery?"

"No, I mean we've gotta get him to a hospital".

"I ain't taking no cop to no hospital," Joe replies, before leaning a little closer. "Well, would you look at that. This here ain't just an ordinary cop, Thomas. This here is Deputy Sheriff Robert Haims".

"Who?" I ask.

"Deputy Sheriff Robert Haims," he continues. "Even by the standards of this fair county, this man is a particularly dumb and nasty piece of work".

"You know him?"

"Asshole booked me a couple of times," he says. "I swear, he had this big shit-eating grin on his face every damn time". He pauses for a moment. "Hey, Mr. Haims. How you doing this fine afternoon? I think my tail-light might be faulty. You wanna book me?"

The cop turns his head slightly toward us and lets out a brief gurgling sound.

"So what do we do?" I ask. "What's wrong with him?"

Joe stares at the cop for a moment. "Go back to the truck," he says eventually.

"Why?"

"Because I say so". He turns to me, and I can see that his mood has changed. That's one of the tricky things about Joe: he can be happy and cheerful one moment, and pissed as all hell the next. Sometimes it's kind of scary to see how he can change on a dime like this. It's impossible to predict how he'll react to anything, but one thing's for sure: this cop has tapped right into the anger at the heart of Joe's black soul.

Reaching into my pocket, I pull out my mobile phone and try calling for help. After a moment, I realize that there's no signal.

"Go to the truck," Joe says darkly.

"What are you gonna do?" I ask.

"I'm gonna do the right thing," he replies.

"The guy's in agony. We can't leave him here to suffer, even if he's a stinking cop. I just don't want you to see what I do. Not up close".

"You mean -" Looking down at the cop, I realize what's about to happen. My first reaction is that this is wrong, that there's no way Joe can do something like this. Then again, maybe Joe's right and this is the best thing. Hell, for all I know, the cop might *want* to die; he seems to be in a real bad way, and it's hard to believe that he'd even survive the drive to hospital. If I was in such a bad state, I figure maybe I'd want it all to be over. There's no point living if you're in constant pain. I learned that from my grandfather, after he spent the best part of two years dying of cancer and begging the doctors to kill him. Still, I don't much feel as if it's Joe's place to decide that this is the right thing to do.

"What are you waiting for?" Joe asks, staring at me darkly. "This ain't no spectator sport. Go to the truck so I can do the humane thing and put this cock-sucker out of his misery".

"Are you sure we shouldn't -" I start to say.

"Go to the truck," he says firmly.

"Okay," I say, taking a step back.

"I always knew I'd end up killing one of these sons of bitches one day," Joe says, rolling his sleeves up in preparation. "I just never pictured it being a mercy killing". He crouches down next to the car and reaches inside, carefully slipping the cop's gun from his holster. Although the cop looks down and watches his gun being removed, he seems powerless to do anything to stop his weapon being taken. I guess he knows what's coming; I just hope he can find some peace with the Lord before he dies.

Sighing, I turn and head back to the truck. Once I'm sitting in the passenger seat, I reach out and tilt the rear-view mirror until I can see Joe standing by the side of the police car. I watch as he wipes the gun on his shirt, and then slips it into his pocket. There's a pause, as he seems to just stand and stare at the cop, and then finally he puts his hands on top of the car, turns his body slightly and kicks the cop as hard as he can. Shocked, I stare for a moment as he kicks again and again, and finally I have to turn away and close my eyes. I hear a crunching sound in the distance, followed by silence. This is a side of Joe I don't want to see. Eventually, I hear footsteps coming closer, and I open my eyes in time to see Joe getting back into the truck.

"Job done," he says with a grin on his face.

"I thought you were gonna shoot him," I reply.

"And waste a good bullet? Fuck, no". He laughs as he starts the engine and gets us underway. "What's wrong, Thomas? You don't hate cops enough to think that was kinda funny?"

I stare at him. All my life, I've looked up to Joe and seen him as a kind of hero, but right now there's a part of me that wants to punch that smile right off his face. He looks so self-satisfied, as if he's just done something worthwhile and noble, when what he just made that guy suffer a painful death. A bullet to the head would have been so much more humane, and at least he could show some degree of compassion. As it is, it seems like Joe finds the whole thing kind of amusing, which makes me wonder whether my brother is in fact some kind of monster. When we set out today, I looked up to him; now he makes me feel sick.

"Don't look at me like that," he says after a moment.

Feeling physically ill, I turn to look out the window. I can't help thinking about that cop, and what it must have been like for him. He was dying, and one of the last things he experienced in his life was Joe kicking his head to pieces. Closing my eyes, I pray that at least maybe he was so far gone, he didn't know what was happening to him. I figure there's no way God would let the man suffer like that, so his death was probably quick and painless. Still, none of that changes what Joe did: I've always seen my brother as some kind of cool rebel outsider, but now I see that he not like that at all. He's a violent asshole who doesn't give a damn about other people. Looking down, I see that my hands are shaking.

# ELIZABETH

*Manhattan*

"ARE THEY BACK YET?"

"No".

"Did you hurt your finger?"

"No".

"There's a bandage on it".

"No".

"Yes, there is".

"That's not my finger. That's my thumb". Turning to Henry, I'm briefly filled with uncontrollable loathing. All he's done, all day, is sit around and watch TV, and then sit around complaining after the power went. Everything's my fault: when the internet's slow, it's my fault; when the laptop overheats, it's my fault; when the power goes, it's my fault. I don't want to be one of those whinging, constantly complaining martyrs who feels put-upon all the time, but right now I feel as if I've had the entire burden of our family dumped onto my shoulders. I can certainly think of things I'd rather be doing instead of babysitting my younger brother for the thousandth time.

"What are you looking for?" he asks.

"Candles," I say, crouching to open another cabinet door.

"What for?"

"Gee," I say, "I don't know. Why do you *think* I want candles in a gloomy apartment, Einstein?" To be honest, I don't think I've ever seen a candle in this entire apartment, but I figure everyone has to have a few floating about, don't they? Even if they're just old, discarded gifts, they'll do for now. After all, my mother seems to keep huge stockpiles of just about every other household item you could imagine: we have boxes of rubber gloves, and whole cartons of cupcake holders, and pile upon pile of plastic party plates with matching plastic cutlery. Just one fucking candle doesn't seem like too much to hope for. So far, though, it's looking like there's nothing. We live in a high-tech, high-cost luxury apartment in the heart of Manhattan but, when push comes to shove, we don't have a candle. At least cavemen could light a fire.

"When's Mom getting back?" he asks.

"I don't know!" I reply, raising my voice. "I don't know, I don't know, I don't know! I'm not a fucking mind-reader! I'm not omnipotent!" Sighing, I stand up and march past him, heading to the window. Looking down at the street, I see a bunch of cars parked in the street, but none of them are moving. It's as if all the drivers have just abandoned their vehicles and decided to walk home instead, although I don't see any pedestrians on the sidewalks at all. Frankly, it's almost like the city is deserted. I keep expecting the lights to flicker back on at any moment.

"Maybe it's the apocalypse," Henry says.

I turn to find that he's come to join me at the window, staring out at the subdued cityscape.

"Don't be stupid," I say firmly.

"I mean it," he says. "If it's the end of the world, they'd probably turn off the power. I mean, why else would it have been off for so long? This is what they'd do in an emergency, to stop people from panicking. They've got experts who know what they're doing, so if they were operating normally, they'd have fixed it by now. Therefore, something's wrong". He pauses. "Maybe someone's blown it up".

"Blown what up?" I ask.

"I dunno. The place where they control everything from".

"You sound just like Mom sometimes," I

mutter. "No-one's blown anything up".

"How do you know?" he continues. "The TV's off. The internet's not working. We haven't got a radio. So how do you know the apocalypse isn't happening right now? Or maybe aliens have landed. It's not like there'd be any way to find out". He pauses. "If the end of the world *was* happening, this is how it'd be. You wouldn't have all the details. Everything'd suddenly stop and no-one would know until it was too late. There'd be, like, nuclear explosions and zombies eventually, but it's not like anyone would go around making sure people know exactly what's happening. There wouldn't be, like, newsletters and stuff".

I take a deep breath. Right now, Henry is being particularly annoying. I mean, he's always *kind* of irritating, but right now he's excelling himself. It's pretty typical of his fucked-up generation to assume that a brief power-cut is a harbinger of total apocalyptic catastrophe. It's like someone's cut the metaphorical umbilical cord that connects him to the grid, and now he's floundering around in sheer panic. I swear to God, if Henry's not staring at a screen, he gets withdrawal symptoms.

"Are you scared?" he asks.

"No," I shoot back.

"You look scared".

"No, I don't," I say. "How the hell would you know what I look like when I'm scared,

anyway?"
"You look like that," he says, staring at me.

"Like *what*?"

"I don't know how to describe it. Just... like *that*".

"Just stop asking dumb questions, okay?" I say, turning and heading through to the kitchen. It's as if, in the absence of any other form of entertainment, Henry's decided to keep himself occupied by following me around and asking me stupid questions. I wish I could hide my irritation better, but unfortunately my lack of tolerance is probably goading him to continue. I just want everything to go back to normal. It's insane how a lack of power and a silent apartment can conspire to make me so nervous.

Suddenly the room shakes. Just for a second, everything seems to rumble, and there's a distant boom. Looking up, I see that the ceiling is shaking, as if something huge just passed straight over us.

"Elizabeth?" Henry shouts from the front room.

"What?" I reply cautiously. The shaking has stopped, and now I'm standing completely still, listening out for any sign of it coming back. I swear to God, it was as if the entire structure of the building was being rocked.

"Holy shit!" he shouts. "Elizabeth, get through here!"

I pause for a moment. "Why?" I ask, even though I can tell from his tone of voice that something's seriously wrong.

"Just come here!" he shouts. "Elizabeth, seriously! You *have* to see this!"

I take a deep breath as I remind myself that I'm older than him, so it's my job to keep him calm until our parents get home. This is what being an older sister is all about, right? Grabbing my glass of juice, I head through to the front room. It's starting to get properly dark outside, and the apartment is getting gloomier by the minute, but there seems to be some kind of bright haze in the distance.

"What is it?" I ask, seeing that Henry's standing by the window. I've got this terrible, growing sense of doom in my chest. Whatever's going on outside, I'm not sure I really want to know. After all, it's clearly not going to be something we can fix, so why should we worry unnecessarily? We need to just stay here, avoid anything that might upset us, and wait for the whole problem to be fixed by the people who are paid to fix things. "What is it?" I say again, loitering uncertainly by the door.

"Come and see," he says, seemingly unable to stop looking at whatever's caught his attention outside. Henry's usually pretty hard to impress, but right now he seems kind of over-awed. The last time I saw him this shocked, it was when he unlocked a hidden level on a video game.

"Why don't you just tell me?" I ask. When he doesn't reply, however, I reluctantly make my way to the window. As soon as I'm standing next to him, I realize what he's looking at. In the distance, almost as far as the horizon, there's a huge fire. Something's burning a few miles out of the city, sending thick black smoke billowing into the darkening evening sky.

"What is it?" Henry asks.

I stare at the flames. "I don't know," I say eventually.

"It's near the airport, isn't it?" he continues.

"Yeah," I say. "I mean, maybe. I'm not sure".

"Mom and Dad -"

"Mom and Dad left the airport hours ago," I say quickly, trying to cut off any unnecessary speculation. Still, I'm starting to shake with fear. "They're in a car somewhere between there and here".

"Okay," he says, "but what the hell *was* that? Was it a plane?"

I watch as the fire continues to rage in the distance. "I don't know," I say. "Maybe".

We stand in silence for a few minutes, just watching the bright yellow and orange fire as it continues to burn. It's kind of hypnotic, in a way; as the city gets darker and darker, while the flame burns brighter and brighter. Whatever's burning, it seems to be fueling a fire of massive proportions.

"You know what else is weird?" Henry asks after eventually.

"What?" I say, still staring at the fire.

"It's been, like, five minutes," he continues, "and I don't hear any sirens or anything".

"Huh," I say. Standing and staring into the distance, I become aware of the room getting gloomier. At this rate, we're going to be in total darkness within the next half hour, and then what the hell are we supposed to do? Glancing back across to the hallway, I close my eyes and find myself hoping and praying that maybe our parents will come walking in at any moment. That's the only thing I can think of right now. If they don't come back through that door soon, I have no idea what we're supposed to do next.

# THOMAS

*Oklahoma*

"THIS IS FUCKED UP," Joe says as he parks the truck in the forecourt of Dan Adams' petrol station. "Where the fuck is everyone?" He looks over at me. "You alright, Thomas?"

I nod.

"What's got your goat?" he asks, grinning from ear to ear. "Today's a good day, kid. Trust me, you go through life getting beat up by cops, you don't often get a chance to turn the tables and show 'em how you feel about 'em. Today was the kind of day that comes along rarely in a man's life". He pats me on the shoulder, before climbing out of the truck. "What's wrong, little brother? We did a good thing back there. That guy was suffering. I put him out of his misery".

"We should call someone," I say. "Let them know".

He shakes his head. "You know what cops are like. They won't understand. They'll lock me up. Don't worry, someone'll find him. Besides, he's dead now, so it ain't like he's suffering. Come on. I'll shout you an ice cream or something. Fill the tank up".

I watch as he struts toward the door that leads into the building. It's weird, but I always used to admire Joe; I used to watch his confident, happy-go-lucky way of walking around, and I'd hope that one day I might get to be the same. In our small rural community, he was always the cool guy. Right now, though, I hate him. I hate him more than I've ever hated anyone in my life. I just don't understand how one human being could be so mean to another. No matter what that cop might or might not have done to Joe over the years, no-one deserves to be killed in such a painful way. Joe had an opportunity to do the right thing, and he went the opposite way instead. I guess he's not the man I thought he was; I guess he's just a thug.

Getting out of the truck, I wander around to the other side and grab the pump, before sticking it into the truck and pulling the handle. For a few seconds, gas starts flowing into the tank, but suddenly there's a grinding sound and the whole damn thing thuds to a halt. I try again and again, but it resolutely refuses to work. Frowning, I put the pump back on the rack and grab the next one, but the same thing happens. It's pretty clear that the whole damn place has been emptied out. In fact, it looks completely deserted.

"There's no-one fucking here!" Joe shouts, coming back out to the forecourt. "I guess the guy's jerking off somewhere. Well, I hope it's worth it, 'cause I ain't paying for no gas when I can get it for free. You done?"

"The pumps are empty," I say.

"What do you mean, empty?" Joe asks, coming over and grabbing the pump from my hands. He squeezes the handle several times, but nothing comes out. "What you do to it?" he asks. "You drop it or something?"

"I didn't do anything," I tell him. "There's no gas".

"Of course there's gas," he replies, slapping me lightly on the back of the head. "This is a gas *station*, dummy". He pulls a frozen ice cream from his pocket and shoves it into my hands. "I got that for you," he says, as he grabs the other pump and finds that it, too, isn't working. "It was supposed to be a reward for your pumping skills, but I guess you can still have it".

"Did you leave some money on the counter?" I ask, looking down at the ice cream.

"Did I leave some money on the counter?" He laughs. "Did I leave some *money* on the *counter*? Yes, Thomas. I left some fucking money on the fucking counter, neatly piled up for Dan Adams himself to find when he gets back. I also left a note, explaining what I'd bought, and a glass of fucking milk in case he's thirsty. Jesus fucking Christ, Thomas. You think this guy doesn't owe us a fucking ice cream after all the years we've been paying over the odds for fucking gas around here?" He slams the pump against the side of the machine, hitting it so hard that the whole thing rattles. "So where's the fucking gas, anyway?"

"I guess no-one filled it up," I say, placing the ice cream on top of the other pump.

"You don't want that?" Joe asks.

"No. I'm not a thief".

He sighs. "Whatever. I'm going back inside to see if I can find out what the fuck's going on. I tell you one thing, though. If we can't get any gas, we're turning around. I'm not risking the trip to town if I don't know we can get back tonight. The one thing worse than spending the night at home would be spending the night in that dump of a town".

Figuring I'm not gonna help him rob a gas station, I walk around the side of the building and take a seat in the dirt, staring out across the field and watching the wind turbines in the distance. I swear to God, there's a part of me that wants to just tell Joe where to stick it, and walk home instead. Sure, it'd take the best part of a week to make the journey, but at least I'd show him that I'm not gonna sit around and watch him act like an asshole. Still, there are probably better ways to make him see that. Maybe I can change him; maybe I can make him understand that what he's been doing is wrong. If he keeps going this way, he's gonna end up being a total, unbearable asshole, but I can't help thinking that maybe he's got a decent heart buried deep within his rotten chest.

Lost in my own thoughts, I barely even notice the sound of an approaching car. I mean, I notice it in the background, but it remains kind of abstract until suddenly the brakes squeal and I realize we've got company. Shuffling over to the corner of the building, I peer back at the forecourt and see a woman stepping out of a small, old car. She looks to be about Joe's age, fairly attractive but with the kind of trampy clothes that people tend to wear in cities. Making straight for the gas pumps, tottering on ridiculously high heels, she tries first one pump and then the other, before slamming them both against the machines in frustration.

"Looking for gas?" asks a familiar voice. Joe emerges from the building, with bags full of cigarettes and liquor in his arms, and a sickening grin on his face. He's obviously feeling pretty pleased with himself right now. I guess for a guy like Joe, this is all his Christmases come at once.

The woman stares at him. She's wearing sunglasses, so it's hard to make out her expression, but she's got bright red lipstick and she seems to have a very still, very calm kind of demeanor. She looks kind of classy, too, so she probably sees Joe as being some kind of rough animal.

"I'm afraid we're all out of gas," Joe continues. "Might have a bit of a party going, though, if you're interested". He glances around, but doesn't seem to spot me as I remain just around the corner. Watching Joe from a distance, it's even more obvious that he's a total sleaze. "Thomas!" he shouts. "Get your ass back here!"

"Who's Thomas?" the woman asks nervously.

"Thomas's my brother," Joe says, leaning against the truck. "He's probably off taking a leak somewhere. The kid's just a streak of piss anyway".

"Is this place shut?" the woman continues.

"Yeah," Joe says. "Kind of. I don't quite know where the owner's gone, but he seems to have taken off at short notice. Pretty inconvenient, huh? I swear, some people just don't have a good work ethic these days. Makes it a lot harder for the rest of us, if you know what I mean".

"Do you know where I can get some gas?" the woman asks. "I'm almost dry". She seems kind of highly-strung and nervous. If someone told me she was a bank robber being chased across state lines, I wouldn't have a hard time believing such a fanciful story. She just comes across as being so skittish and strung out.

"You don't look dry," Joe says with a smile. "There's no gas here. Place is clean out".

"Just like every place I've passed since yesterday," the woman replies.

"Seriously?" Joe laughs. "Well, then we're all fucked. If the gas stops flowing, civilization's gonna collapse down around our ankles by dinnertime, isn't it? There'll be fucking riots in the streets". He pauses for a moment. "I'm sorry, M'am. I didn't mean to use such coarse language".

"The roads are pretty empty lately," she continues, glancing back the way she came. "I swear, you're the first people I've seen in two hundred miles".

"Is that a fact?" Joe asks.

"Do you have any gas I can borrow?" she replies.

Joe sniffs. "Got some at home".

"Where's that?"

"Not too far. You got enough gas to cover about ten miles?"

"Maybe".

Figuring I have to go out front eventually, and realizing I can't take any more of their inane back-and-forth banter, I wander around the corner and head over to the truck. Frankly, the last thing I want to do is hang around while Joe makes flirty small-talk with some random woman, but I figure he might cut it out a little if I'm sitting right there. My best bet is probably to just wait it out, let him fuck her around the back, and then hope that he's content to turn around and head home.

"Here's my little brother right now," Joe says. "Thomas, this is... Huh, you know what? I don't think I know this fine lady's name".

"Lydia," the woman says.

"This is Lydia," Joe says, turning to me. "That's a nice name, isn't it?"

I shrug as I get into the truck and pull the door shut.

"You'll have to excuse Thomas," Joe continues. "He doesn't really know how to treat a lady. He hasn't been versed in the finer side of life. He ain't as experienced as the rest of us".

"I guess he's just a kid," she replies.

"Fuck you both," I mutter under my breath.

"Well, Lydia," Joe continues, "I've got a suggestion for you. If you like, you can follow us back to our place tonight. We live on a farm with our parents, but don't let that put you off. I have my own room, and it's kind of separate from the rest of the house. It's not exactly the lap of luxury, but you can join us for dinner, and I might be able to swing you some spare gas. My Dad's a farmer, so he has plenty stored away for a rainy day. How does that grab you?" He waits for a reply, but the woman seems hesitant. I don't blame her; if she's got any kind of sleaze-radar, she should have taken a pretty instant dislike to my brother. "It's not a trick question," Joe says eventually. "It's an offer. You don't have to take it, but it's the finest hospitality you'll get around here for a fair few miles". He rattles the bottles he just stole from the gas station. "If you like a drink," he adds, "we've got that covered too".

Lydia smiles. "You think I'm the kind of girl who'd just follow a strange guy home?"

"I'm not strange," Joe says. "Give me a chance, I'll prove it. Anyway, I figure you've got no choice. You need gas".

She pauses for a moment. "I guess," she says eventually, though she's clearly dubious. I don't blame her; I mean, it'd be pretty stupid for her to just come back to our house, but maybe she's desperate. Hell, maybe she's dumb! "But I've got a gun in my bag," she adds, "and I'll use it if you try anything".

"Okay," Joe says, banging the side of the truck before coming around to the driver's side. "I like a girl who's direct and to the point. You just follow us and we'll be back at our place before sundown. Deal?"

Without saying anything, Lydia turns and gets back into her car. Joe climbs into the seat next to me and starts the engine. From the grin on his face, it's pretty clear that he thinks he's gonna get some action tonight. For the sake of my faith in humanity, I hope he's wrong. I hate the idea of a guy like Joe getting lucky so easily. He doesn't deserve to get any action at all.

"I swear to God," he says with a smile, I'm gonna tap that ass tonight if it's the last thing I ever do. I wouldn't even mind if I keeled over from a heart attack right after, you know what I'm saying?" He smiles as he waits for me to say something. I guess he thinks I'm gonna look up to him and think he's a hero; the truth, though, is that he's starting to make my skin crawl. "Yes, Sir," he continues after a moment, "you'd better wear ear-plugs in bed tonight, kid, 'cause I'm gonna make the house shake 'til morning. I hope you're proud of your older brother".

"Why would she sleep with *you*?" I ask, staring out the window. "She's pretty. She's not gonna get into bed with some redneck fuck-wit she meets at the side of the road".

"Watch your mouth," he replies.

"I suppose you could always tell her about the cop," I say, turning to him as he steers us onto the main road and we set off, with Lydia's car following close behind.

"What do you mean?" he asks.

"The cop you killed," I say. "You could tell her about that. You know, just to turn her on. Just to really impress her".

He doesn't reply. Instead, he just keeps his eyes on the road and we drive on in silence for a few minutes.

"Shut up," he says after a few minutes of silence, and that seems to be the limit of his interest in talking about the matter.

# ELIZABETH

*Manhattan*

THERE'S A SHUFFLING SOUND from the other side of the door, followed by a kind of clinking noise as Mrs. DeWitt opens the spyhole. An old lady who lives alone, she usually keeps herself to herself, and I don't think I've ever actually spoken to her properly before. This isn't the kind of building where people stop and chat socially in the hallways and elevators; it's the kind of building where people get on with their own lives and rarely extend the pleasantries beyond an occasional polite nod. Still, she's the nearest neighbor we have, and I figure she might have a little more experience with this type of situation.

"Who's there?" she calls out. "I can't see a

damn thing. It's too dark!"

"It's Elizabeth Marter from down the hall," I say, standing in the pitch-black corridor. I wait for her to reply, but there's nothing. It's so weird being here not only in complete darkness, but also complete silence. No air conditioning hum. No sound from the elevators. Nothing. I never realized before how noisy the building could be, even at night. "I just came to see if you know when the power's coming back on," I continue eventually. "It's been a while now".

The door opens and a bright stream of torchlight shines directly in my face.

"I don't have a clue," Mrs DeWitt says. "How would I know? The way things are going, I wouldn't be surprised if we have to live the rest of our lives like cavemen".

"Well, I -"

"Did you hear that blast out somewhere near the airport?" she continues, apparently oblivious to my attempt to reply. "What the hell's going on? It sounds like there's a god-damn war starting up".

"I don't know what that was," I say, still a little disorientated by the light she continues to shine in my face. I've got my hands up to cover my eyes. "I don't know anything. That's why I came to ask you. I just thought you might have heard something".

"I was asleep this afternoon," she says.

"Woke up about five and found everything was off. Cooker. Toaster. Refrigerator. Television. Lights. Everything. No juice in any of them. It's coming to something, isn't it, when you can't even rely on the electricity company to keep the juice flowing. I don't know what they do with all the money we pay them, but they sure don't spend it on keeping things running properly. Probably goes straight in their pockets".

"The power cut out just after lunch," I tell her. "My parents are still out at the airport. I don't know how long it's gonna take them to get back here, but I think the traffic's pretty snarled up".

"Of course it is," she replies, sounding annoyed at me. "The lights are all out. No-one can see a damn thing. The whole city's probably come to a standstill".

"Just hold tight and wait it out," she says. "Aren't your parents home?"

"No," I say, "they're -" I suddenly remember that I've already told her that my parents are at the airport, so I don't see there's much point in going over everything again. This conversation is going round and round in circles. "I'm sorry I disturbed you," I say finally, stepping back from the doorway.

"Just stay calm," she continues. "Stop waiting for everyone else to solve your problems. A little darkness never hurt anyone. Hell, it might even do you good. You kids are pampered these days".

"Okay," I say quietly, as she slides the lock back across. "Thanks," I continue once I'm alone in the corridor. "Sorry to bother you. Have a nice evening". I pause for a moment. "Go fuck yourself," I add quietly.

Turning, I wander back along toward our apartment. Feeling my way slowly and carefully to the door, I suddenly hear a noise somewhere nearby. Stopping, I stare into the darkness; sure enough, I hear the noise again: it's a kind of clicking, shuffling sound, accompanied by a hushed tone that sounds like someone breathing nearby. I don't want to get paranoid, but I could swear that it sounds like someone's standing a few meters away. Frankly, with the lights out, there could be someone just inches away from me and I wouldn't know anything about it until I felt their breath on my face.

"Hello?" I say quietly, feeling stupid for even vocalizing my fear. This is just my mind playing tricks on me in the dark.

"Hey," says a male voice.

My heart nearly leaps out of my mouth as I realize that I'm not alone. That voice wasn't Henry; it sounded like an older guy. There are a whole bunch of people living in this building, but I've never really met or spoken to any of them. We tend to mostly not really talk to our neighbors. The weird part, though, is that Mrs DeWitt is the only other person who lives up here on the top floor, so I don't see why anyone else would be wandering about in this corridor at all. My mind immediately starts racing as I think of all the things this guy could be: a burglar, or a murderer, or someone with a knife, or -

"You okay there?" the voice continues after a moment. Suddenly I see a small pen-light shining in the darkness; after a moment, it flashes in my direction, as if the person is trying to get a good look at me.

"Yeah," I say, my heart still pounding in my chest. "I'm fine".

"Okay," he replies. "That's good".

I wait for him to say something else, but he just continues to shine the pen-light at me.

"Do you want something?" I ask.

"No," he says. "I was just coming up to make sure that everything's okay with you folks. With the lights out and all, you never know what might be happening".

"Yeah," I say, trying to sound polite even though all I want to do is make my way past this guy and get back to Henry in our apartment. "I'm just going back home," I explain, hoping against hope that the guy will realize that I want to be left alone. I mean, I don't want to sound rude or paranoid, but at the same time I'd really rather just get back to my brother.

"I'm just a neighbor," he says.

"A neighbor?"

"From downstairs".

"Oh". I wait for him to go away, but his penlight remains pointed straight at me.

"You're Elizabeth Marter, right?" he says.

I pause for a moment. "Yeah," I say eventually.

"Thought so. I've seen you in the lobby a few times. We haven't actually spoken, but, uh, I like to maintain a good understanding of who lives in the building at all times. Helps in case I have to spot an intruder". He pauses for a moment. "How old are you?"

"Me?" I pause for a moment. "Twenty-two," I say eventually, which is a lie. I'm almost twenty-one, but I figure I should try to make myself sound a little more formidable.

"Twenty-two, huh? Nice age".

"Yeah," I mutter, still feeling for the door. I'm starting to wonder whether I've gone too far, or not far enough; either way, all I can feel is the wall, until suddenly my hand brushes against something soft and I realize it's the man's arm. I pull back.

"You've got a brother, right?" the man asks, shining the pen-light directly at my face.

"Yeah," I say.

"How old's he?"

I pause. "He's also twenty-two," I say after a

moment.

"He is? Are you twins?"

"No," I reply. "Why?"

"Just thought you might be, if you're the same age".
"We're not".

"Huh". He pauses, and then he sighs. "I don't know, I've seen the both of you about, I thought he looked a lot younger. Well, I just came up because I heard someone moving about. I figured you might be in trouble, or something, what with the lights being off and your parents being out of town and everything".

"No. I'm fine. We're fine".

"Huh. Well, that's good to hear".

I wait for him to say something else.

"I should probably -" I start to say eventually.

"My name's Bob," he says suddenly, interrupting me. "Bob Sullivan. I live downstairs. Right below your family, I think. I'm in number seven. I've seen you about. I don't mean to creep you out, but I'm the kind of guy who keeps his eyes and ears open. I doubt you've spotted me. Slightly older guy, a little overweight maybe, not quite so much hair as I used to have. I'm usually coming home about five. I wear this big military-style jacket. Navy Seals, that kind of thing".

"Sorry," I say, "I don't think I've seen you".

"That's okay. I like it that way, to be honest. Being anonymous and stuff like that. I tend to just head in and head out pretty quickly. What about you?"

"What *about* me?"

"Do you like to draw attention to yourself? Like, with what you wear and stuff? Tight clothes, jewelry?" He sniffs. "Tattoos, things like that".

"No," I say, taking a deep breath. "Look, I don't mean to be rude, but I really need to get back to my brother now".

"I'll help you," he replies. "This way, right?" I see the pen-light change direction, pointing down the corridor and briefly flashing across our front door at the far end.

"I..." I pause for a moment, desperately trying to think of a way to get him to just leave me alone. Finally, I realize that the best approach might simply be to accept his help and then get inside the apartment as quickly as possible. While this guy is undeniably being weird, I'm probably overreacting. After all, just because someone's a little pushy and socially awkward, they're not necessarily dangerous. My mother always tries to make me scared of people in the city, but I should try to overcome her paranoid indoctrination and accept some help when it's offered.

"Come on," he continues, as the beam from his pen-light shines along the corridor. "It's not far to your door, is it?"

"No," I say, taking a deep breath before walking forward. I head straight for the end of the light, which already seems to be dancing over the door-frame that leads into our apartment. I can sense the man walking alongside me, and I can hear him breathing, but at least he doesn't seem to be trying anything. At least with the beam of light stretching out ahead of us, I can be certain that he's not looking at me.

"Here you go," he says as we reach the door and he shines the pen-light at the bronze number. "I told you I'd get you back, safe and sound". "Thanks," I say, pushing the door open.

"If you need anything," he continues, "anything at all, just come down to apartment seven and knock on the door. Or, you know, you could just bang on your floor and I'll probably hear it. Sometimes I can hear from below if you're banging stuff about up here".

"Sure," I mutter, turning to shut the door. "Thanks again, I -"

"Elizabeth!" Henry calls out from the front room. "Who are you talking to?"

"That's your brother, huh?" Bob continues. "You got more than one?"

"No," I say cautiously. "Why?"

"Oh, no reason. I just didn't think he sounded like he's twenty-two, that's all. Sounds more like a teenager. I guess it can be hard to tell sometimes".

"Well, that's him," I say.

"Your parents home?" he asks.

"Yeah," I say.

"Huh. I thought they were away for the weekend. I saw them leaving with suitcases". He starts to push his way into the apartment. "Maybe I should -"

"No!" I say firmly, pushing the door almost into his face. "Thanks, but we're fine!"

He pauses. "Okay," he says finally, with a shrug. "If you say so".

"Sorry, I really have to get going. Thanks for the help". Before he can say anything else, I push the door shut and take a deep breath. I hear the sound of Bob walking away down the corridor, and moments later I hear the stairwell door swinging open and then closed. Finally, he's gone. I feel kind of bad for assuming the worst about him, and I'm sure he was only trying to help, but there was still something about him that made my skin crawl. After taking a moment to calm down, I slide the chain across on the door, for extra security. Just in case.

# THOMAS

*Oklahoma*

"HE'S NOT THERE!" I say, staring into the police car as we drive back past.

"Sure he is," Joe says, keeping his eyes on the road. "He's just flat on his back on the front seats. Dead as a doornail".

"No," I say firmly, turning to keep my eyes on the vehicle. "I swear, he was gone. If you don't believe me, pull over".

"Bullshit," Joe replies. "Trust me, if you'd seen how I left him, you'd know".

"It's not bullshit! He must have got out and walked off!"

"Well, I'm not stopping," he continues. "Fuck that shit".

I watch as Lydia's car continues past the scene, keeping pace with us. "I guess you *can't* stop," I say. "I mean, how would you explain it to your new girlfriend? Hey, darling, here's the cop car where I crushed a dying man's skull earlier".

"I knew I shouldn't have let you come". He pauses for a moment, and finally I realize he's staring not at me but at something in the distance. "Fuck, that plane's flying low".

Following his gaze, I see a large airplane traveling roughly parallel to us, only a few hundred feet off the ground. It's so low, you'd think it was coming in to land, and although it's perhaps a kilometer away, it's still the closest I've ever been to one of the damn things.

"Do you think it's okay?" I ask.

"How would I know?" he replies. "I'm not a fucking pilot".

As we keep going, it becomes increasingly clear that the airplane is continuing to lose altitude. It's still going pretty fast, and it's maintaining a course that keeps it well within sight of our truck, but this definitely isn't normal. After a moment, I realize I can just about hear the distant roar of its engines, and they sound as if they're spluttering slightly.

"There's not a landing strip around here, is there?" I ask.

"No," Joe replies flatly. He sounds worried;

usually, he'd start making jokes, but this time he seems more interested in keeping an eye on the airplane as it continues to get closer and closer to the tops of the trees.

"Is it crashing?" I say.

As we continue to watch the plane, it starts to brush against the tops of the trees. The body of the jet seems to wobble slightly.

"Holy fuck," Joe says, "I think it's gonna come down".

"No way," I say, feeling my chest tighten with fear.

"Fucking way!" he shouts, just as the plane starts crashing through the highest part of the forest. It's barely a couple of hundred meters from us now, and it's starting to tilt slightly. Joe keeps his foot on the accelerator as we watch the plane start to bump a little as it continues to hit the trees; finally, it tips to one side and all we can see is a wing, before the entire plane disappears from view. There's a moment of calm and silence, and then there's a huge crashing sound, like metal and wood being ripped apart.

"Did that -" I start to say, but suddenly there's a massive explosion, sending a fireball up into the evening sky. The whole area seems to shake for a moment, and Joe's truck skids a little before he brings it under control and pulls over by the side of the road. Once the shaking has subsided, the fireball starts to dissipate as it rises higher and higher, but now there's a thick plume of black smoke coming from a spot in the forest where the airplane came down.

"Jesus fucking Christ," Joe says. "That motherfucking thing just crashed right in front of us". As the words leave his lips, there's a second explosion, almost as loud as the first. The ground shakes again. "Fuel," Joe continues. "That must have been the fuel coming up". There's a third explosion, and we sit there wide-eyed as the smoke starts to thicken by the second.

"What do we do?" I ask. My heart's pounding so hard, I reckon it could leap out of my chest at any moment, and I've got this cold sweat all over my body. "Do you think there might be survivors?" When he doesn't reply, I turn to him and see that his face is completely pale. It's almost as if he might faint at any moment. My heart racing, I turn to look back at the horizon; there's already a lot more smoke than before, most of it pitch black. Suddenly there's a banging sound on my window, and I turn to see that Lydia has come over to the truck. Reaching out, I wind the window down.

"What the fuck just happened?" she asks, still wearing her sunglasses. It's weird, but she still sounds slightly bored and whiny, almost as if she's interpreted the crash as a personal affront to her own plans.

"Well, I think a fucking plane just crashed," Joe says.

"Yeah," she replies, "I think you're fucking right". She sighs. "I guess we need to call someone. Is your phone working? I just tried mine and I haven't got any signal". She drops her cigarette and swears as she bends down to pick it up. "Fucking fuck," she mutters, grabbing a lighter from her pocket and trying to relight the tip.

Joe grabs his phone from the glove compartment and tries to bring up a number, but after a moment he puts it back down. "No signal," he sighs. "Boy, the wonders of the digital age, huh? No damn signal to be had for begging. I've always said, you can't trust modern technology, not when you're in a jam". He smiles awkwardly; it's sad to realize that even in the aftermath of a huge accident, he still seems to be trying to impress Lydia.

"Huh," Lydia replies, clearly not impressed by either of us. Her hand are trembling as she continues to try, in vain, to get her cigarette lit again. "So what are we gonna do about it? Just, like, drive on or something?"

Joe opens his door and steps out of the truck, walking around and standing in the middle of the road. In the distance, smoke is still rising up from the forest, and it looks as if there's a fire raging. From here, things don't look so bad, but it's hard not to imagine the carnage that must be going on at the scene.

"What the fuck's going on?" Lydia mutters, still trying to relight her cigarette. "It's like the whole fucking world's just falling apart today. It's just a fucking lighter, for fuck's sake". Frustrated, she throws her lighter against the side of the truck and it bounces to the ground. "You got some matches?" she asks.

I shake my head.

"Huh," she replies. "I guess I might have some". She turns and starts walking back to her car; moments later, however, she stops and there's a pause before she drops to the ground.

"Joe!" I shout, getting out of the car and running over to Lydia's fallen body. I remove her sunglasses and immediately see that she's sporting a massive, slightly swollen black eye. Whatever caused that, she got it long before she met us. "She was fine!" I shout, my hands shaking as I check her pulse. She's still alive, but that black eye looks alarming. "She was just going to get some matches from her car!" I tell Joe as he kneels next to us.

"It's okay," Joe he says, rolling her onto her back "She fainted, that's all," he continues. "Probably shock". He checks her pulse. "She's fine. She just needs to rest for a bit. Grab her legs and we'll get her in the back of the truck". Together, we manage to get her over to the truck and settle her flat on her back in the rear compartment. "We're gonna have to get her home," he continues. "We'll come back for her car later. Right now, she needs to get to bed. It's probably just shock from seeing a fucking plane come down, that's all".

"Shouldn't we try to wake her up?" I ask.

"How do you wanna do that?" he replies. "Stick her nose in your armpit? She'll come round when she's ready. Right now, we need to call someone and make sure they know where this fucking plane's come down. Maybe the land-line's working again".

"They'll know," I say. "They have to know. They'll have seen it on radar".

"Whatever," Joe replies, rushing back to the driver's seat. As soon as I'm back in the truck with him, he slams his foot on the pedal and the wheels screech before we head off along the bumpy road. Nearby, smoke and flames are continuing to rise into the sky, and after a moment I realize that the road is gonna start curving in the direction of the crash-site.

We carry on in silence for a few minutes, until suddenly a large piece of mangled fuselage comes into view up ahead. Joe slows down and carefully drives around what turns out to be a big chunk of torn metal, with steam rising from its surface. It quickly becomes apparent that the road is dotted with bits and pieces from the accident, although the actual crash-site is about a hundred meters to the right. As Joe picks his way between the twisted pieces of junk, I can't help staring at the flames that are raging in the forest. There's a kind of dusty mist everywhere, and small pieces of black ash are drifting down from the sky. Looking up, I see bits of metal and plastic strewn through the trees, with pieces of torn fabric hanging from the branches like macabre decorations.

"Fuck!" Joe says suddenly.

I look ahead and see that there's a seat to the side of the road. It's upside-down and on its front, but there appears to be a human leg dangling off from one side, and it's obvious that there's a body still strapped in. Nearby, there's a lump of burning metal. Joe carefully drives us around both items, but it's hard not to stare at the seat and think about the person who was sitting there. Just an ordinary person on a plane, and now he's dead on the side of the road.

"Ain't this the stuff of fucking nightmares?" Joe says quietly.

"I don't get it," I reply. "Why did this happen?"

"How the fuck should I know?" he replies. "It's nothing to do with us. We just gotta call it in and make sure they know about it. They've got people who'll come and investigate. Like, they'll be searching for the black box and stuff like that. Haven't you seen those documentary channels?" He sighs. "Fuck, this place is gonna be crawling with people soon, poking about and trying to find out what happened. Media, too".

We keep going, and I'm pretty sure I can see several more seats among the trees. It looks like the plane broke up when it crashed, scattering the seats far and wide. Eventually, however, it becomes clear that there's a little less debris on the road up ahead, and after a few minutes we seem to be through the worst of it. Eventually, Joe parks the truck by the side of the road and we sit in silence. It feels like we're supposed to do something, but neither of us knows *what.* It's not as if we're remotely equipped to deal with the aftermath of a plane crash, and there's clearly no chance of anyone having survived; at the same time, it feels as if it'd be wrong to simply drive away.

"Dear Lord," I say quietly, closing my eyes and lowering my head, "we pray to you that the souls of these -" Suddenly, I realize Joe's laughing. Opening my eyes, I turn to him.

"What the fuck are you doing?" he asks, with a big grin on his face.

"People died," I point out. "I thought -"

"Do what you want," he mutters, grabbing his phone and getting out of the truck.

"Where are you going?" I shout.

"Just getting a couple of videos," he says, using the phone to record the fire. "I might be able to sell this footage to one of the networks for some serious cash. They'll have to credit me, too. Imagine that. Footage from my phone being shown all over the world".

Sighing, I realize that even when he's just witnessed something as shocking as a plane crash, Joe's mercenary side kicks in and he starts looking for a way to make some money. Seriously, I just wish he's react like a normal human being, instead of standing there and recording a series of videos. I turn and take another look at Lydia, but she still seems to be out cold. I guess it's for the best; she was obviously totally shaken up by what happened, so she might as well stay passed out until we make it back to the farm. Turning back to look out the window, I see that Joe has moved a little closer to the edge of the road, presumably she he can get some better shots with his phone. I stare blankly at him for a moment, before finally I have to admit the truth to myself: today's the day I finally started to hate my brother.

# ELIZABETH

*Manhattan*

"IT'S STILL BURNING!" Henry calls out to me. He's standing by the window, having barely moved an inch since the flames first appeared a few hours ago. It's almost as if he *wants* there to be something wrong, as if he hasn't quite understood that this isn't a video game. "Elizabeth," he says after a moment.

"It's still burning".

"That's great," I reply. I'm sitting on the sofa, using the light of my phone to read a magazine. While Henry seems to be enjoying the drama, I've been trying to take my mind off what's been happening. Since my encounter with Bob Sullivan in the corridor, I've forced myself to calm down and stay positive. I'm fairly certain that things are going to be okay: the power will come on eventually, and our parents will walk through the door at any moment, and the explosion in the distance will turn out to be some mundane consequence of the blackout. I mean, it's just insane to think that these things won't happen. This is twenty-first century America; there are people out there who are working to fix things, and in a day or two we'll sit around and laugh about all of this.

"It must be fuel," Henry continues. "Wouldn't most other stuff have been, like, totally burned out by now?"

"Probably," I say, flipping a page in the magazine.

"Why would they let it spread? Why wouldn't they get out there and stop it? And where are the sirens?" He waits for me to answer. I guess he hasn't realized that I'm doing my absolute best to block his voice out of my mind. "Elizabeth, why wouldn't they put it out?"

I sigh.

"Elizabeth? Why wouldn't they put it out?"

"I have no idea," I say, as my phone flashes up a 'low battery' warning. Great. Why didn't I put it on charge last night? Putting the magazine down, I bring up my mother's number and try calling her again, but nothing happens. It's as if the entire phone network is down, which is kind of scary. I mean, even if there's a blackout in New York, the phones should be working. I guess maybe the network's been restricted to emergency calls only, so the police and fire teams can communicate; then again, Henry's right when he says it's odd that there are no sirens. It's as if everything's stopped.

"What are you doing?" Henry asks after a moment.

"Nothing".

"You trying to call Mom?"

"No".

"Who were you trying to call?"

"No-one".

"You were. I saw you".

Sighing, I turn the phone off. There's no point wasting battery when it looks like we might have to go a few more hours without power. Once the screen blinks off, I find myself sitting in total darkness once again. At least I've got the pen-light as back-up. Glancing across the room, the only hint of light comes from the window, where I can just about make out the outline of Henry as he stares at the distant fire, which is giving the horizon a dull orange tinge.

"Is there anything out there at all?" I ask eventually. "Like, any lights anywhere?"

"No".

"Not even in the distance?"

"Just the fire".

"Any flashing blue lights?"

"No".

I sit in silence for a moment. How can it be that after almost half a day, the whole of New York is still without power? Seriously, there are people who are paid to make sure that things like this don't happen. There must be back-up systems, and secondary back-up systems, and yet everything's gone totally wrong. I hope someone gets completely fired for letting something like this happen. I mean, people might die if there's no power soon. It's pitch-black out there, so how are people meant to find their way around. I guess car headlights are gonna work for a while, but it's still pretty insane to think that the city seems to be out of control. I mean, if that Bob Sullivan guy *had* turned out to be dangerous, what would I have been able to do? It's not like I can call the police. The longer this blackout goes on, the more worried I'm starting to get. I still have faith, though, that everything's going to work out in the end.

Suddenly I feel the room starting to shake again, and there's a loud rumbling sound from above.

"Another one?" Henry asks, unable to hide the fear in his voice.

"It's different," I say, as the furniture starts to vibrate all around us. "It's closer".

"I don't see anything!" Henry says, staring out the window.

Getting up from the sofa, I walk over to the window and stare out at the dark city.

"It's getting louder," I say, feeling the vibrations against the soles of my shoes. In fact, everything is shaking: the floor, the walls, the furniture, the window, the ceiling. Everything. I swear to God, even the fillings in my teeth are starting to rattle. I can't shake this overwhelming feeling that something terrible is about to happen.

"It's coming from above," Henry says. He looks up; there's just enough moonlight for me to be able to see his face, and his eyes are wide with fear. "Do you think it's -" he starts to say, before suddenly there's a huge roar and something large and bright flies directly over our building, just a hundred or meters or so above the roof.

Blinded by the bright lights for a moment, I shield my eyes as the whole building shakes so hard, it seems as if it might collapse and send us tumbling down into the street. Finally, the sensation passes and I see that the object that passed over us was an airplane.

"What the fuck!" Henry shouts.

"It's okay," I say quietly.

"It's not fucking okay!" he shouts.

"It's okay!" I shout. "It's going to be okay!"

We watch as the plane banks to the right, as if it's trying to avoid the buildings. With the rest of the city still completely dark, the plane is easy to pick out as it veers first in one direction, and then another. Finally, it disappears behind some buildings for a few seconds, before there's a huge explosion. A fireball bursts in all directions, and once again the building shakes. Wherever the plane went down, it can't have been more than a few blocks away. Henry grabs my arm as the building continues to vibrate. After a moment, I hear a cracking, splitting sound; at first I'm not sure where it's coming from, but finally I realize it's the glass in the window.

"Get back," I shout, suddenly pulling him further into the room. A fraction of a second later, the window shatters, sending a shower of glass toward us. Fortunately, however, we just about miss the worst of it. Finally, the shaking stops and we're left standing in shocked silence, with an icy wind blowing through the broken window. In the distance, a huge fire is raging in the heart of the city.

"See?" Henry says, looking excited as the distant flames light up his face. "I was right. It's the end of the world".

# DAY 2

# THOMAS

*Oklahoma*

"HEY," SAYS JOE, wandering into the kitchen. He seems tired, and kind of deflated, as if the events of the day have finally taken a toll on him. He loiters by the table, waiting for me to reply, but I'm not interested in talking to him; I just carry on carving the piece of wood I brought in from the shed earlier. With the power still off, this is literally the only interesting thing I can find to do. I'm not even good at carving, so all I'm doing is cutting off little chunks and hoping that it'll eventually look like something. I'm not tired, though, so I figure I'll sit here until the candle burns all the way down to the stump.

"So you're not talking to me now?" he asks,

grabbing a beer from the fridge and cracking it open. "Seriously? I just get talking to Dad again after God knows how many years, and now you clam up on me, huh?" Again, he waits for me to respond, but I refuse to even look at him.

"The rest of us have been talking it over," he says eventually. "We're gonna fill the truck up in the morning and head to Scottsville. This power-cut's gone on for too long, and Dad's starting to get worried. I told him what Lydia said, about Scottsville being deserted, and he said he didn't believe it. I could tell it got to him, though. Truth is, when Dad's worried, *I* get worried". He takes a sip of his beer. "You noticed that the fire's still burning in the distance? No sirens, no nothing. It's as if that fucking plane crashed and no-one's noticed".

Trying to get another piece of wood off the block, I accidentally let the knife slip. The blade nicks the end of my thumb, slicing the skin slightly.

"You cut yourself?" Joe asks.

"No," I spit back, watching as a bead of blood starts showing through the split in the skin. Determined not to let Joe see that I fucked up, I carry on carving.

"You a liar now, boy?" he says.

I continue to ignore him.

"I hate what you did," I say.

"What I did when?" He sounds genuinely shocked, as if he doesn't understand.

"Today". I put the carving down and, finally, I look at him. "I hate the way you pissed on that man when he was dying, and then I hate the way you stole that stuff from the gas station, and then I hate the way you were taking videos of the plane crash like it was some kind of freak show. And I hate the way you were looking at that Lydia woman, like you were so sure you were gonna get her into bed!"

"Woah!" he says, feigning surprise. "Where did all that come from?"

"Don't you care about other people?" I ask. "Don't you care about what God's gonna think of you?"

"God?" He laughs. "Sweet Jesus, Thomas, do you really believe in that stuff?"

"You shouldn't have done what you did," I say, staring at him. I shouldn't have mentioned God; Joe always reacts badly to that kind of talk. I'm not surprised; he probably knows he's already done enough bad stuff to guarantee he's gonna burn in hell.

He smiles. "Yeah, well... I move in mysterious ways, kid". He pauses for a moment. "And I don't owe you or anybody an explanation. Just remember that whatever I did to that fucking cop, it was the result of years and years of built-up frustration where I didn't have any way to fight back at people like him. When they get their teeth into you, there's nothing you can do to make them let you go. Nothing. And they've got the full force of the law behind them, backing them up and patting them on their fat little heads and telling them that they're right. So yeah, when I saw that guy today, I did something dumb and mean. And you know what? It felt good. And you know something else? I'd do it again. Because they've been shitting and pissing on me for years".

He takes a deep breath. "She's fine, by the way, in case you were wondering".

"What?"

"Lydia. She's fine. I assume that at some point, in-between judging other people and praising the Lord, you might actually find a moment to ask how another human being is getting along?"

"I'm glad she's fine," I reply sourly.

"Looks like she just fainted," he continues. "Mom took her some food up to the spare room. She seems pretty embarrassed about the whole thing, but I reckon she'll be absolutely fine tomorrow. I guess we'll just give her some gas and she'll be on her way, although I wouldn't mind if she stayed for a few days. She's pretty hot. Besides, she seems to have a cold or flu or something, so maybe she'll be in no fit state to drive away". He takes another swig from his beer bottle. "So what does your God reckon is going on right now?" he asks eventually.

"What do you mean?"

"The power's gone out. That plane came crashing down out of the sky. Apparently fucking Scottsville is a ghost town. Does your God have anything to say about all of that?"

"They'll fix it tomorrow," I say firmly.

He smiles. "Okay, kid. I'm gonna let you believe that. Anyway, you might be right. I hope you are". He sits opposite me, placing his beer bottle on the table and starting to peel the label away. "Sure feels like something's going on, though".

"You not going to bed?" I ask.

"Not yet," he says, still picking at the label. "You?"

I shake my head.

"Truth is," he continues, "I don't much want to fall asleep. After all that stuff we saw today, I don't know what I'd dream about. Burning bodies and jet fuel and bits of wreckage. I don't want to have to have those kinds of nightmares".

I take a deep breath. The weird thing is, I feel the same way. At the same time, I don't want to get into some big conversation with him about what's happening, because I still hate him. Instead, I go back to carving my chess piece, while Joe sits quietly and drinks his beer. This goes on for almost an hour before, finally, I get up and - without saying anything - I turn and head up to bed. When I get to the top of the stairs, I pause for a moment to listen to the sound of Lydia coughing in the distance, and then I head through to my room.

# ELIZABETH

*Manhattan*

OPENING MY EYES, I stare up at the ceiling and try to pretend that nothing's wrong. It's not actually that difficult: sunlight is streaming in through my bedroom window, and it could almost be just another normal day in Manhattan. The electricity *could* have come back on, and the taps *could* be working again, and my parents *could* have finally got back from the airport. All these things *could* have happened, and we might end up sitting around and laughing about how crazy things got.

Except...

I know things aren't back to normal.

I know because of the noise.

My bedroom is completely silent. No air

conditioning. No computer. No noise of any kind. And there's no noise from outside, either. To be honest, I never noticed all the little background noises until they were gone, but now it's seriously creepy to be flat on my back in bed and surrounded by a wall of nothingness. I just want it all to come back; any moment now, the power could be restored and suddenly the air conditioning would click back into action, and my computer would beep as it starts up again, and then the front door would open and my parents would come storming back with tales of their nightmare overnight stay at the airport, and I'd finally be able to apologize to my mother for being mean to her the other day...

Looking over at the table on the other side of my room, I see the birthday gift that's waiting for my mother. She and I have been arguing all the time lately, but I was hoping that maybe I could make things better by getting her this big glass teapot that I saw in a store downtown. It seems kind of pathetic now, but that teapot was supposed to be my way of showing her that I care about her. If she never comes back, she'll never know that, and I'll never get to apologize. Even if this is the end of the world, I hope she at least gets home and sees the teapot. I keep imagining the smile on her face when she sees it. *If* she sees it.

After a few minutes, I get out of bed and wander through to the front room. The first thing I notice is that it's freezing cold in here. The window broke last night, and a cold breeze is making the curtains flutter. There's glass all over the floor and, with the lights still off, the whole room seems strangely dull and gray. There's dust everywhere, presumably from the huge cloud that was sent into the sky when the airplane that hit the ground. Grabbing my mother's over-sized winter coat from the hallway, I figure I might as well stay warm. I slip a pair of shoes onto my bare, sockless feet and finally I make my way across the broken, dusty glass until I'm standing at the window.

The fires are still burning. There are two on the horizon, and there's one in the city itself. For whatever reason, it looks as if three airplanes crashed yesterday, and no-one's gone to help. No sirens, no fire teams, nothing. They've just been left to burn. Finally, turning my head a little, I realize I *can* hear something after all; I can hear the crackling of the flames from a few blocks away, still burning. It's a very faint sound, but in a strange way it's kind of reassuring; at least *something* is making a noise, and I figure that sooner or later someone's gonna turn up to sort everything else and put things back to normal.

"Hey," says a voice behind me.

Turning, I see my brother Henry standing over by the door to the kitchen. He's noticeably calmer and quieter than usual; by this time in the morning, he'd normally be watching cartoons and eating cereal, but he seems to be just standing there, waiting for me to say or do something. He's got this slightly dazed look in his eyes.

"Hey," I reply. "Did you manage to sleep?"

He shakes his head.

"Me neither," I say. It seems crazy that we even *tried* to go to sleep, but at the time I thought it was the best thing to do.

"It's cold in here," Henry says.

"Yeah," I say quietly.

I smile, before leaning out through the window and looking straight down at the street below. Even from all the way up here on the top floor, I can see that there's not a soul in the streets. I guess everyone has decided to stay inside and wait for help to arrive. You'd think that maybe people would spill out onto the sidewalk, trying to find out what's going on, but it's almost as if the whole city has taken fright.

"When do you think the power's gonna come back on?" he asks.

I shrug.

"But it *is* gonna come back on some time, right?" He waits for me to reply. "Elizabeth?" He waits again. "It'll probably be today," he says eventually. "People are gonna be so mad about all of this. Do you think someone did it deliberately?"

I shrug again.

"I think it was," he says. "I think this was all caused by someone who, like, got into the systems and made it all happen. Probably some idiot in his bedroom managed to get past the security in some network, and switched everything off".

"Maybe," I say, although I can't help wondering why it's taking so long to fix. I can kind of just about believe that someone could fuck things up like this, but I don't understand why it would take forever to get the city back to normal. Surely there are people outside New York who can see what's happening? Why don't they come and help? It's as if all the people you'd expect to fix the problem have, instead, just given up.

"So where do you think they are right now?" Henry asks.

"Who?"

"Mom and Dad. Do you think they're at the airport?"

I shrug, feeling as if there's no point saying anything else. The truth is, we can stand here and speculate all day, but we don't *know* anything. We can guess, but it's all just a load of bullshit. With no internet, no TV, no anything, we're just standing here and waiting for something, anything, to happen. For all we know, this could be a simple fuck-up by the power company, or it could be something worse. It could be some kind of crippling computer virus that's shut everything down, or it could be a nuclear disaster, or it could be some kind of plague. Hell, it could even be a zombie apocalypse. The point is: we have no information. We're alone up here on the top floor of an apartment building, and we don't know a damn thing. We're also completely, hopelessly helpless.

"The freezer's leaking," Henry says after a moment.

I turn to him. "What?"

"The freezer's leaking. There's no power, so the ice has started to melt. There's, like, a puddle on the kitchen floor". He pauses. "I just thought you should know".

"Why should *I* know?" I ask.

He stares at me, and that's when it hits me: the realization that he thinks I'm in charge. Henry's always hated it when I'm left to look after him, but right now - with everything going crazy - he's naturally just waiting for me to do everything. I guess it makes him feel better to think that in some way I'm here for him, and that I know what to do, and that I'm going to make sure things are okay.

"I'll take a look in a minute," I say, even though I have no idea what I'm going to do. I guess I'll have to take out the food and see what's still good and what's not, and then I'm gonna have to work out what we can eat for breakfast. Fortunately, the fridge was pretty well-stocked when our parents went away, so at least we won't starve. We can eat kind of normally today, and the power has to come back on by evening. I mean, no matter how fucked up things are going to get, at some point someone out there is going to get on with the job of reconnecting everything. This can't last forever.

"Should we go outside?" Henry asks suddenly.

I pause for a moment. "No," I say eventually. "We're not going outside. You never know what it's like out there".

"Don't you wanna see the crashed plane?"

"Not really".

I wait for him to argue with me, but he just stares out the window. He's trying to act normal, but he can't quite manage to pull it off. The normal Henry wouldn't ask me if he could go outside; he'd just head out the door. It's kind of weird, the way he's deferring to me. Weird and scary, since I don't know what the hell we're supposed to do. Going outside would be a mistake, though; I'm certain of that. The best thing is just to sit tight and wait for help, because at some point I *know* that help will arrive. The worst thing to do would be to panic and start running out into the street. We're must better off staying up here, because this is where we're safe. As long as we're in our apartment, nothing can hurt us. That's the theory, anyway.

# THOMAS

*Oklahoma*

FOLLOWING THE NOISE OF banging and hammering, I find my father around the back of the barn. He's working on the truck, fixing a few things and filling the tank with gas. At first, he doesn't seem to notice that I'm here, which is typical: he's lost in his own world of wing-nuts and gaskets, where every problem can be solved with the right tools and a few tightened screws. Eventually, however, he glances over, and I realize he's probably been aware of my presence all along.

"You come to help?" he asks.

"What do you need?" I reply.

"Pass me the wrench from over there".

I grab the wrench and hand it to him. "Are

you going to Scottsville today?" I ask.

"That's the plan. Gonna get to the bottom of this mess. Power's still out, and I don't like that. I need to make sure things are under control. You know what people are like. They're probably running around like blue-assed flies, trying to work out what to do. They need a good, firm hand to get things in order".

"Huh," I say, watching as he continues to work on the truck.

"Something on your mind?" he asks eventually.

"I was just wondering what's happening," I say. "Do you think it's something serious?"

"A plane falls out of the sky?" he replies. "That's serious in my book".

"Why hasn't anyone gone to look?" I ask. "Do you think no-one's noticed?"

"I'm sure the people on the plane noticed," he replies. "I'm sure the people in *charge* of the plane noticed too, and the people waiting at the other end for people to arrive". He pauses for a moment. "About five years ago, there was a nasty car wreck on that stretch of road. Some tourist family had a blowout and went head-first into a tree. A man, a woman, and a few kids. All dead, and one of 'em even got dragged half out of the window by a wolf. Anyway, within three hours there were ambulances and police in the area. You could hear the sirens from here. Three hours, that's all. And yet that plane's been down for more than half a day, and there's nobody come to take a look".

"You worried?"

"I'm taking a pragmatic view of the situation," he replies. "Something's off, and only a fool would sit around and wait for other people to fix it. Now get in the truck and fire her up. See if she's running okay".

Leaping at the chance to actually do something useful, I hurry around to the side of the truck and climb inside. I turn the key to start the engine, but it splutters and eventually dies; I try again, but the same thing happens. "What's wrong with it?" I ask.

"Fuel pick-up," he says, leaning back under the hood. "Okay, get out again".

I climb out of the truck. "It was okay yesterday".

"No," he sighs, "it was struggling yesterday. Like most things around here, it was getting by, despite a few major flaws under the hood. Normally, I'd let it keep running until it breaks, but I figure if things aren't so ordinary out there, I need to make sure this thing's rock-solid reliable before I head off to Scottsville. After all, I can't be calling a tow truck without any phone signal, can I?" He checks his watch. "If it gets much later, I might have to stay the night. It might be just you and your

Mom and your brother here until the morning. That'll be fun for you".

"And Lydia," I reply.

"Huh," he says, clearly not impressed. "Isn't she heading off pretty soon?"

"I'm not sure," I say. I pause for a moment, feeling a little reluctant to mention what I heard when I was leaving the house just now. "I don't know if she's okay," I add eventually. "I think she's maybe a little sick".

"Sick in what way?"

"Coughing".

He pauses. "Yeah. I heard her in the night".

"I think I heard her in the bathroom too".

"Now what were you doing listening to a woman's bathroom noises, son?"

"It's right next to my room," I reply. "I think she was throwing up".

"Is that right?"

"She seems worse this morning," I continue. "Mom's gonna take her up some honey tea, but..." My voice trails off as I wait for my father to say something, but he seems lost in thought. "I just keep wondering if she's okay," I continue. "She seemed fine yesterday, and then last night she fainted and then she started coughing and it just seems like she's getting worse and worse". I glance back over at the horizon, where smoke is still rising. I feel as if there's some thought in the back of my mind, some fear that I'm keeping squashed down; it's as if, in the pit of my stomach, I feel like things are a lot worse than they seem. "Joe says she's just got a cold," I say quietly.

"Try the engine again," he says.

Getting back into the car, I turn the key, but the engine still won't start up properly.

"Okay, okay," he continues, "that'll do. Don't want to cause more damage". He leans back under the hood, and I stay sitting in the front of the truck. Opening the glove compartment, I see that Joe has already removed the gun that he took from the dying cop. Great, that's all we need: Joe with a handgun.

"Lydia came through Scottsville," I say, raising my voice so he can hear me. "She said it was empty. She said there was no-one there at all".

"Well, maybe she's delirious," he replies, laughing. "I've been going to Scottsville my whole life, and I can tell you that the place is always pretty busy. Where, exactly, would all those people go?"

I take a deep breath, imagining Lydia wandering the empty streets. All morning, I've been mulling this situation over in my head, trying to work out what might have happened. Taking everything into account, I've come to the conclusion that something pretty bad might have happened on a major scale. In fact, whenever I think of Lydia walking through a deserted Scottsville, I can't help picturing dead bodies hidden away in the buildings. I guess I've always had a hyper-active imagination, thanks to spending my childhood growing up out here on the farm, but something tells me there might be something bad happening. First there was the power-cut, then the abandoned gas station, and now news of Scottsville being empty. I feel as if there's some huge puzzle, and I need to start fitting all the pieces together.

"Are you sure it's a good idea to go to Scottsville?" I ask eventually.

"A good idea?" He pauses. "It's never been a particularly good idea to go to Scottsville, son, but it's the nearest town. Beggars can't be choosers. Guess I'm just gonna have to grit my teeth, get in and out as fast as possible, and hope I don't run into too many idiots. Not gonna be easy, mind. Scottsville's about 95% idiots".

"That's not what I mean," I continue. "What if..." I take a deep breath. "What if she was right, and the place is deserted. I mean, why would she make that up?"

"Don't be dumb, son," he replies. "The people of Scottsville aren't gonna just up sticks and vanish, no matter what some streak of piss girl claims. I don't know why she'd say something like that, but frankly I don't give a damn. She can spout off whatever gibberish she wants. She's feverish. Probably imagined the whole thing. What she says doesn't change a thing. I've been going to Scottsville all my life, and the worst thing that ever happened to me was a dose of the clap. Why should things be different this time?" Stepping back, he slams the hood down. "Try it again," he adds.

I turn the key, and this time the engine starts up perfectly. Say what you like about my father, but he's a damn good mechanic.

"Okay," he says, patting the front of the truck. "Let's go get something to eat".

After taking one final look at the truck, I climb out and then I follow my father along the dirt path that heads around the barn. It's odd, but because I know that all the power's off, I feel like everything looks and feels much calmer. I suppose that's all in my head, but I swear to God I can feel that the crackle of the wi-fi isn't in the air, and there are no mobile phone signals bouncing off the surfaces. The only sound is the dirt under my feet, and then the gravel as my father and I get closer to the house. As I stop at the door and remove my shoes, however, I hear another noise. I look up at the window of the spare room, where Lydia sounds as if she's coughing her guts up. All those germs, spreading out from her mouth like a great big, infectious cloud. I can't help worrying that her sickness might be something serious. Hopefully I'm wrong, though. Hell, like my father says, I'm wrong about most things. Then again, something feels different this time. All my life I've dreamed of running away from the farm and starting a new life somewhere else. What if I've left it too late, and now the rest of the world isn't even there anymore?

# ELIZABETH

*Manhattan*

CLEANING UP THE MESS takes a while, but it feels good to be actually doing something. Henry and I move all the furniture out of the front room, and then we use a dustpan and brush to sweep up as much of the dust and glass as possible. We can't get it *all*, of course, and there's this stupid moment when I automatically reach for the vacuum cleaner before remembering that there's no power. No matter how carefully we try to sweep up all the dust, it seems as if there are always more particles to be found, and we have to take regular breaks due to the cloud of ash that keeps developing in the room. Eventually, though, we decide that we've done a good enough job, so we move all the furniture back into place and stand in the doorway, covered in dust and ash, and staring at the results of our hard work.

"We need to fix the window," I say after a moment.

"How?" Henry asks.

"I don't know," I reply, before suddenly a bright idea hits me. "Come on," I say, turning and heading through to our parents' bedroom. It doesn't take too long to find a bed-sheet that's big enough to cover the window, and we use some thick tape from the craft drawer to seal it in place. The sheet's white, but it still blocks out quite a lot of light, and as we once again stand back to admire our handiwork, I can't help wondering if we should have just left the window open. I mean, it's just air that was coming in, right? Still, at least this way we'll probably be able to stay a little warmer.

"Okay," I say, turning to Henry. "We might be in for a few days like this, so we're gonna sort ourselves out. Are you cold?"

He nods.

I lead him back through to our parents' bedroom, and we gather up all the spare blankets and duvets we can find. Eventually, we've built a fairly impressive little fort that should, hopefully, keep us warm. After we've both put on several more layers of clothing, I take Henry to the kitchen and fix up a salad from the stuff in the fridge. It's definitely not something that Henry would normally eat, but he seems happy enough, and as we sit at the bench and eat in silence, it's almost as if things are getting back to normal. It feels kind of good to have taken charge and actually done something; at least I know we're not gonna starve or freeze to death up here.

"You wanna go on the roof?" Henry asks when we've finished eating. "The roof?" I stare at him. "Why the hell would I want to go on the roof?"

Smiling, he runs through to our parents' bedroom. I hear him banging around in there, looking for something, and finally her returns with a pair of binoculars.

"Where did those come from?" I ask.

"I noticed them earlier," he replies, "when we were looking for sheets. I think they're the ones Dad uses when he plays golf. We can see for miles with these things".

"It's gonna be cold up there," I point out.

"We'll wrap up," he says, clearly recovering a little of his usual enthusiasm. "Come on, Elizabeth, we need to know what's going on. With these, we can get an idea of how far the blackout's spread and what's happening in the distance".

I open my mouth to argue with him, but finally I realize that maybe he's right. It *would* be good to get a general view of what's going on, and at least we'll be safe up on the roof.

"Okay," I say, shrugging. "But not for long. Seriously, Henry, it's gonna be freezing up there, so maybe put on two coats".

It takes me a few minutes to find a key so I can lock the door, but soon we're wandering along the corridor and heading up to the roof. The elevators are out of action, of course, so we take the emergency stairs. It's kind of weird to be doing this, but at least we're doing *something*; it already feels like a million years since the power was working, and I'd go crazy if I had to spend the whole day cooped up in the apartment. I guess my attention span is pretty much shot to pieces.

"Remember to prop the door open," I say to Henry as we step out onto the roof. He hurries over to the edge, so I have to grab a nearby bucket and use it to prevent the door from closing behind us. The last thing we need, right now, is to get stuck up here. Taking Henry's phone from my pocket, I switch it on and wait for it to power up. I know it's a long shot, but I can't help hoping that maybe the phone network's back up and running by now. Unfortunately, after a few minutes of waving the phone in the air, I have to accept that there's not going to be any signal. Sighing, I turn the phone off, put it away, and walk over to join Henry.

"Jesus, it's cold up here," I say, as the wind blows gently around us. The folds of my coat are flapping slightly, and in normal circumstances I'd never stay outside like this. "You see anything?" I ask.

"Nothing," he replies, using the binoculars to scan the horizon.

"Oh well," I mutter. "Worth a try".

"No," he says, handing the binoculars to me. "I mean, I see nothing. That's what I see. A whole lot of nothingness. Nothing moving, no-one doing anything. See for yourself".

When I take a look through the binoculars, I see what he means. The freeways are all dead, packed with stationary cars. There's no sign of anything or anyone moving about, although I'm pretty sure I can make out the vague shapes of people sitting in some of the vehicles. I train the binoculars on one particular car and try to see if the person in the front seat is even moving, but when I try to zoom in, the image gets too blurry.

"Where is everyone?" Henry asks.

I don't reply. I turn and look toward the airport, where two separate fires are still raging. Again, though, there don't seem to be any people there at all. It's almost as if everyone just vanished.

"What if there was an evacuation?" Henry says.

"Why would there be an evacuation?" I ask.

"Hey," Henry says, tapping my elbow, "what's that?"

Lowering the binoculars for a moment, I see that he's pointing at a nearby building.

"What's *what*?" I ask.

"The window on the top floor, at the end," he says. "There's someone in there, on the floor".

I train the binoculars on the window, and I immediately see what he means; there's a male figure, wearing black trousers and a white shirt, flat on his back on the floor. I turn the dial on the binoculars, which allows me to zoom in a little, and I realize that there's something slightly odd about his face, as if his complexion is a little pale or even slightly yellow.

"Is he dead?" Henry asks.

"I don't know," I say quietly.

"Give me the binoculars".

"In a minute". I need to get a better view of the man, because right now he looks to be dead. I mean, I already knew that there must have been deaths during the blackout, thanks to the plane crashes, but I've never seen a dead body before and now I'm feeling really strange and blank. There's definitely something wrong with the man's face, as if his skin has turned the wrong color, and I've got this mounting series of dread at the thought that this clearly isn't a coincidence. I've been wondering all morning about the strange lack of people in the streets, and now this dead body hints at the possibility that maybe there's something more serious than a blackout.

"Give them to me!" Henry says, trying to grab the binoculars from my hands. I struggle to hold onto them, and somehow we contrive to both let go; I turn and watch in horror as the binoculars fall over the railing, plummeting down the side of the building.

"Well done!" Henry shouts angrily, shoving my arm. "What did you do that for?"

"If you hadn't grabbed them -" I start to say.

"Idiot," he spits at me, turning and walking back over to the door.

"Hey!" I shout, following him into the stairwell. "I was going to give them to you if you'd just waited a few more seconds!"

"So instead you decided to toss them over the side," he replies, pushing the door open and heading back into the stairwell.

"Don't blame me!" I reply, keeping up with him. "You're the one who grabbed them!"

"We need to go outside," he replies, storming through the door and into the corridor. "We should go and find out what's happening".

"No," I say firmly. "We're staying in the apartment. If something's wrong, we should just stay right where we are and not take any risks".

"Like that dead guy in the other building? He stayed inside, and he's still dead!" He stares at me. "We're not safe up here. We're not safe anywhere.

What if that plane last night had been slightly lower? It would have hit us and we'd be dead. Sitting around here isn't going to help. We should go out and see if there's anyone who knows anything".

I shake my head.

"You can't stop me," he says, turning and heading through to the corridor.

"You can't go out there!" I say, running after him. "We just have to sit tight and wait for help to arrive!"

"Help's not arriving," he says, hurrying to our apartment and heading inside. "If we sit around here, we'll just starve".

"You're not -" I start to say, before suddenly stopping. I turn and look down at the door handle. "I locked it," I say quietly, before looking over at Henry as he starts putting on a pair of socks. "Henry," I continue, "I locked the door".

He glances back at me. "You must've got it wrong," he says.

"No," I reply, turning to look across the hallway. "I double-checked it as we left". I reach into my pocket and pull out the key. "You saw me. I locked this door".

# THOMAS

*Oklahoma*

"SHE SOUNDS SICK," my mother says, looking up at the ceiling as we sit down for lunch. Having spent the whole morning pottering about in the kitchen, it's clear that she's concerned about Lydia's continued deterioration.

"Of course she's sick," Joe says, sounding as if he's already anticipated the conversation. He grabs a bread roll and places it next to his soup. "I *told* you she's sick. Why's it such a mystery? People get sick all the time. You get sick, you act sick for a while, and then you get better. It's not rocket science".

"I think it's flu," my mother continues, turning to my father. "I took some food up for her earlier, and she was an awful color. We need to be very careful and wash our hands". She looks over at me. "You keep out of her room altogether, do you understand? I don't want her germs spreading to the entire family".

At the head of the table, my father starts to laugh. "Sounds like it's gonna be a fun old time here while I'm in Scottsville. It'll warm the cockles of my heart to be sitting in some old bar down there, thinking of you lot bickering about some sick bint in the spare room. Just try not to kill one another, okay? I'd hate to come home and find a bunch of corpses littering the house".

"There's nothing wrong with her!" Joe replies, raising his voice a little. "Apart from being sick, I mean. She's perfectly nice. She's a really good person. You've just seen a bad side to her, that's all. You've seen her all snotty and sick, but she scrubs up real well. Wait 'til she's better, you'll see what I mean".

"Are you sure you want to go to Scottsville today?" my mother asks, turning to my father. "Perhaps it'd be better to wait until things are more settled?"

"I want to find out what's going on," he replies. "Besides, I need some supplies. I sent these two off to get some wire yesterday, and they came home empty-handed".

Upstairs, Lydia launches into another

coughing fit. We sit in silence for a few minutes, listening to the sound of her hacking and hacking, and I'm pretty sure that everyone else can tell that she's sicker than just flu. Every time I hear a sound coming from the spare room, it seems to confirm my theory that there's some kind of sickness going around. After all, everything seems to fit: it's as if there's been some kind of virus or plague that's caused everything to go crazy. I've read a lot of books about things like that, and I know the signs. I just wish the others would realize too, though I know I can't raise the subject; they'd just dismiss me as some kind of fantasist. I'm rarely taken seriously in this house.

"That poor girl," my mother says quietly as Lydia continues to cough.

"She's not doing *that* badly," my father replies. "Sitting in someone else's bed, eating someone else's food. If you ask me, she's doing okay. In fact, I might try to get myself a similar kind of arrangement while I'm in Scottsville". He smiles at each of us in turn, as if he's waiting for one of us to start laughing. "Jesus," he mutters eventually. "Tough audience".

"Her throat must be so sore," my mother continues. "I hope she managed to keep the soup down. I left a bucket by the bed with some diluted bleach in the bottom. If she gets much worse, I think maybe we should consider calling a doctor".

Everyone sits silently for a moment, as Lydia's coughing gets worse.

"And how're you gonna do that?" Joe asks eventually.

"She's gonna do herself an injury," my father says. "If she's not -"

"Is this all you've got to talk about?" Joe says suddenly, sounding angry. "Seriously? A fucking jet plane crashes a few miles away, and there's no power, and all hell's going on, and you're happy to just sit here and gossip about some girl's health?" He pauses for a moment. "Jesus fucking Christ, she's sick, but she's not dying! Give her a couple of days and she'll be fine. She just needs to rest. If you want to worry about something, worry about the fire that's still burning out there".

"That's a long way off," my mother says. She clearly doesn't like Joe's outburst, but she knows better than to confront him. In fact, our parents generally let Joe get away with things like this, because they want to avoid a bigger argument. It's a strategy that sometimes works, but most of the time Joe just ends up storming out, and things stay the same. I wish they'd just force the issue and make him leave, instead of tolerating his behavior. The problem is, they've spent the past twenty-something years accepting Joe's stupidity and allowing him to shoot his mouth off; they know it's too late to suddenly start trying to change him now.

"Leave Lydia to me," Joe continues. "I don't want you wasting any of your valuable time looking after her okay? I'll take the food up to her, and I'll change her bucket, and I'll make sure she's okay. You don't have to lift a finger. She'll be out of here in a few days. Hell, maybe I'll go with her".

"Please," I whisper under my breath, although I immediately feel a little bad; after all, it'd be unfair for Lydia to have to put up with Joe's shit. Anyway, even if he *did* leave, he's be back sooner rather than later. That's just how it goes around here.

"I'd hate for you to have to lift an extra finger," Joe mutters.

"Don't talk to your mother like that," my father says.

"I'm full," Joe replies, standing up and walking out of the room, slamming the door closed as he goes. Moments later, the front door slams too, which means he's gone off to sulk outside somewhere. I swear to God, Joe acts like a spoiled teenager. Turning to look at the window, I can see him slouching off toward the barn.

"I think you'd better stay here, Thomas," my father says eventually. "I know you wanted to come to Scottsville, but I'd like you to stay and keep your mother company. I don't know that it'd be a good idea to leave her alone while we've got company, and your brother clearly isn't going to be much help".

I nod. To be honest, I'm kind of glad not to have to go into town; in fact, I'd like to dissuade my father from going, but he seems determined to go and find out what's going on. The thought of leaving my mother alone to deal with a sick girl and an angry Joe is pretty hard to stomach, though, and I guess the best option is for me to stick around. Anyway, I've got a good track record of being wrong about things, so I'm sure my father will come back from Scottsville tomorrow and report that everything's okay. I just need to keep from getting paranoid, and the first step is to stop seeing lines of causation between coincidental, random events. I'm smarter than that.

"Are you definitely staying overnight?" I ask.

"Probably. At this rate, I won't be done until it starts getting dark, and I don't much fancy driving home past midnight. I'll just park up behind Snooty's or somewhere, take a nap, and head on back in the morning. I'll be home about this time tomorrow, all being well".

"Remember we might still be without phones," my mother points out. "So don't go taking long detours. If you're not back by late tomorrow, I'll send Joe and Thomas out to look for you".

Getting up from the table, my father stretches and then grabs his empty bowl so he can take it to the kitchen. "Don't worry about me. I'm fine, it's -" He stops speaking as Lydia coughs again. I swear, she's sounding worse and worse. I've heard people with bad coughs before, even with whooping cough, and this sounds different; it's as if she's trying to bring up something that resolutely refuses to come out. Even if I'm wrong about everything else, I still think Lydia needs to get some medical attention. The last thing we want is for her to die up there in our spare room. Looking over at my mother, I can see from the look in her eyes that she's thinking something similar. She knows this is more than just flu, even if she doesn't want to admit it yet.

"Poor girl," my mother mutters.

"Come on," my father says, turning to me. "You can carry some stuff out to the truck for me".

"Yes, Sir," I reply, getting up and following him through to the hallway. Lydia's still coughing upstairs, and I keep picturing that cloud of bacteria getting bigger and bigger. I figure I might head out to the barn after my father's gone, and look for anything I might be able to use to keep the sickness from infecting the rest of us. I'm pretty sure there's an old gas mask hanging around somewhere; it might sound extreme, but at this rate, I figure we need to take every possible precaution.

"Don't worry," my father says, smiling as he pats me on the back. "This time tomorrow, everything'll be back to normal".

I sit and put my shoes on, while my father wanders to the truck. I wish I could believe him, but - as Lydia continues to cough upstairs - I can't shake the feeling that things are getting worse and worse.

# ELIZABETH

*Manhattan*

"MOM?" I SHOUT, hurrying through to the front room. There's no-one there, but I swear to God I locked that door. "Dad!" I call out, running to their bedroom. Still no-one. "Where are you?" I shout, convinced that they must have come back. After all, they're the only other people who have a key to the door.

"They're not here," Henry says, coming through from the kitchen.

"Then who unlocked the door?" I ask, my heart racing. There's got to be some kind of mistake. I head over to the closet, pulling the doors open. Maybe they're hiding? Maybe they're waiting to jump out and surprise us?

"You obviously didn't lock it properly," Henry says. "Think about it. That's the only thing that makes sense".

"I locked it," I say.

"You're losing it," Henry says, heading back through to the kitchen. "You're really losing your mind. You know that, right?"

I take a deep breath, determined not to snap at him. *Someone* unlocked that door. I know I locked it properly; I remember turning the key, and I remember double-checking. There's no way I'd just go out and leave the door open, but I don't understand who could have come into the apartment. We were only up on the roof for a few minutes, but I guess the most logical explanation is that our parents must have come back, found we weren't here, and then gone off to look for us. Why the hell didn't it occur to me that they might do that? We should have left a note.

"They were here," I say, hurrying back through to the front room. "They must have assumed we were gone, and now they're looking for us. We have to stay here and wait for them to come and check again".

"It wasn't them!" Henry says, standing with the fridge door open. He pauses for a moment. "Elizabeth... Come and see this".

"What is it?"

"Just come and see". He turns to me.

"Someone was here, but I don't think it was Mom and Dad".

Walking over to join him, I look inside the fridge and immediately see what he's talking about. Earlier, we had food and bottles of water. Not much, and not enough to last more than a few days, but we had something to keep us going. Now, however, the fridge is completely empty. Someone clearly came in, cleaned us out and left. I look over at the drawers, which have been opened; it's the same story with the cupboards. Whoever was here, they took every food item in the entire apartment.

"Who the hell did this?" I ask, stunned.

"Looters?" he suggests.

"There are not looters," I reply.

"We need food," Henry says. "I know you don't want to go outside, but we need food. We can't just sit here and starve".

"We're not going to starve," I reply.

"What are we going to eat?"

"We'll find some food," I say, although as the words leave my mouth I can already tell how weak they sound. The truth is, I *don't* know what we're going to eat. Our parents left a prepaid card we could use for buying food while they're away, but with no power in the city, I don't see how we can use it; even if we can find a shop that's open and that hasn't been completely cleaned out, we need some actual cash. "Go to your room," I say, forcing myself to stay calm, "and see what money you can find. Anything, even the smallest coins".

"Why?"

"So we can buy food!" I say, raising my voice. "Go!"

"That's not what we need to do!" he replies. "We need to go and find the people who came in and took the food we already had! They can't have got far!"

"We need to find some cash," I mutter, hurrying past him and heading to my bedroom. "We can't go confronting anyone. We just need to make sure we've got some money". As soon as I'm in my room, I start going through all my drawers, desperate to find some coins and notes.

"You can do what you want," Henry says, standing in the doorway and watching my frantic search. "I'm gonna go and find whoever took our food, and I'm gonna make them give it back. They're probably going door to door, stealing from every apartment".

"Yeah?" I ask, as I start going through the pockets of my old jeans. "You and whose army, Henry?" When he doesn't reply, I look over and see that he's already gone through to another part of the apartment. I hear him in the kitchen, and then finally I hear the front door open. "Henry!" I shout, racing through to the hallway just as he heads out into the corridor. The first thing I see is a large knife in his hand. "What the hell are you doing?" I ask, my heart racing.

"I'm gonna get our food back," he replies.

"What the fuck?" I say, grabbing his arm and pulling him back into the apartment. "Are you serious? You're gonna get yourself killed!"

"No-one steals from us," he says. "They think they can just come into our house and take our food. I'm gonna show them that we're not gonna just roll over and let them do it".

"Excuse me," says a nearby voice.

Turning, I see a man standing in the doorway. He's middle-aged and a little overweight, with a receding hairline and a curious smile on his lips.

"Who are you?" I ask, grabbing the door in case I need to slam it shut.

"Uh, we met yesterday. I'm Bob, from downstairs. It was kind of dark, so I guess you didn't get a look at my face".

I stare at him for a moment. "Hi," I say eventually.

"I couldn't help overhearing you two arguing from downstairs. Thin floors are so thin, you know? Anyway, I think there's been a bit of a mis-understanding regarding the items from your refrigerator. They've been taken to a central hub down in the building supervisor's office". He pauses. "I'm the building supervisor, in case that wasn't entirely clear. Given the circumstances, I used my skeleton key to enter all the apartments and commandeer any food that I could find. Seeing as you weren't here when I came, I kind of assumed you'd gone".

"You took our food?" I say, still finding Bob to be a little creepy.

"Yes, M'am," he replies, "and it's all safe downstairs in the office. Now, I'll gladly bring it back up to you, but what I'm proposing is that, instead, we all pool our resources while we wait for this situation to pass".

"Give us our food back," Henry says.

"I can certainly do that," Bob says, glancing down at the knife in Henry's hand. "I absolutely wouldn't want to cause any trouble. Like I said, I figured you'd left the apartment. Most of the building is empty right now, thanks to whatever it is that's caused all this, so there was just a misunderstanding". He smiles cautiously. "If you're interested, those of us who are still around have decided to have a little meeting down in the office in a while. We figured we might be better off if we have a kind of group approach to things. Pool our resources, you know?"

"Pool our resources?" I reply, a little confused.

"We want our food," Henry says firmly.

"Why don't you just come on down to the

office with me?" Bob continues. "You can see what we've got in mind, and if you still don't like it, I'll help you carry your food back up myself".

Henry turns to me.

"Okay," I say, taking a deep breath. I figure we might as well find out what's going on down there. Bob might be right; if this 'situation' is going to last much longer, we need to have a more effective approach. It might be days or even weeks before everything's back to normal.

"Okay?" Henry asks, looking a little surprised.

"Okay," I say. "We'll go and see what they're talking about".

"Like I said," Bob continues, "this has all been a mis-understanding. I hope you'll come down in about half an hour and we can all talk things over. I figure folks have got to stick together when times are rough, huh?"

"Yeah," I say. "We'll be there". As Bob turns and walks away, I shut the door and turn to Henry. "We might as well see what they're talking about," I tell him. "We've got to go down to fetch our food anyway, so we might as well see if we can learn anything. They might know more about this situation".

"I'm not giving up our food," he replies. "It's *our* food".

"I know," I say. "I just think we need to play

things a little smart".

He stares at me for a moment. "I'm taking the knife with me. For protection".

"Henry -" I start to say, but he turns and heads through to the bathroom. I figure there's not much point arguing with him; he'd just become more determined to do things his way. I'm starting to worry about Henry, since his mood seems to be swinging quite dramatically from one extreme to another. I guess he's scared, but things are only going to get worse if he insists on throwing his weight around. I just need to manage him a little, and make sure he stays calm while we wait for things to get better. At least it's starting to look as though there's light at the end of the tunnel; from what Bob said, it sounds as if people are getting organized, which means we're not on our own anymore. Maybe I'm being a little premature, but I think perhaps we've passed the worst point.

# THOMAS

*Oklahoma*

I CAN STILL hear Lydia coughing as I stand on the porch and watch the truck heading off. I don't like the idea of my father heading to Scottsville, but at the same time I have this calming voice in the back of my head, constantly telling me that it's going to be okay. After all, my father's the kind of man who never gets into too much trouble. Even if there's a problem, he'll find a way to get through it, and I'm fairly confident that he'll be back tomorrow, hopefully with tales of Scottsville being fine and fully populated. Finally, things'll start getting back to normal. He'll have a bunch of stories about all the shit that's been happening, and we'll be able to laugh about how we all started to get worried.

Lydia, though, is another matter.

Looking down at the gas mask in my hand, I realize that I'm going to have to take extra precautions. The mask is an old one, left behind by my grandfather. It's made of thick, dark green rubber, with two large glass eyepieces and a long, snout-like protuberance over the mouth, which I guess is where the filters are located. I remember him explaining that it was from the Second World War or something like that. I'm not entirely certain that it'll protect against infection, but I figure it's worth a try. If nothing else, it's going to be fun to wear it, since the damn thing looks terrifying.

As I head inside, I can hear Lydia's coughs getting worse and worse. I've been around people with bad coughs, but this sounds like something else. It's as if she's convulsed with a need to constantly hack up her guts. I doubt she can keep even a simple meal down, and it's getting to the point where she might even strain her heart. If the internet was working, I'd start looking up her symptoms in an attempt to work out what's wrong; as it is, I have to make do with the meager bookcase in the front room. Unfortunately, my family has never been particularly bookish; I've always kind of stood out in that regard, but we don't have anything that could help diagnose the problems that Lydia's facing.

Heading through to the kitchen, I find my

mother ladling some soup into a bowl. I can tell immediately that she's planning to take it upstairs to our guest, and I'm struck by a determination to make sure she doesn't get exposed to the infection.

"I'll take this," I say, quickly placing the bowl onto a tray.

"No," she replies, "it's fine. I can do it".

"Look," I reply, holding up the gas mask for her to see. "I found it in the barn. I'm gonna wear this when I take the tray in".

"Don't be silly," she says, almost smiling. "Isn't that your grandfather's old thing?"

"You'd rather I don't wear it?"

"I don't want you going in there!" she insists.

"It won't fit you," I point out.

She pauses. "Make sure it's on properly, okay? Even the smallest gap could make the whole thing useless".

"It's okay," I say, turning back to her. "I won't catch whatever she's got. Besides, if one of us has to get sick, it's better if it's me. At least that way, you can make sure everything's okay. If you catch it, Joe and I are gonna end up starving".

She stares at me for a moment. "Wash your hands thoroughly after you've been in there," she says eventually, already starting to wipe down the surfaces. "There's antiseptic cream in the bathroom, so make sure you get every trace of that room off your hands, do you hear me? And try not to be in there for too long. Don't breathe too deep".

"I won't," I say, hurrying out of the kitchen and making my way up the stairs. To be honest, I'm quite surprised that she let me take the tray to Lydia at all. I expected a much tougher fight, but I guess she's being pragmatic: it's true that she's the member of the family who's least dispensable right now, since my father went away, and it's also true that the gas mask might be a little too small for her. When I get to the top of the stairs, I immediately put the tray down and take a moment to fix the mask over my head. It's pretty weird once it's on: I can't see too well, and I can hear my own breathing really loud, and everything smells of dust. Still, it's better than nothing.

I pick up the tray and gently push Lydia's door open. She's rolled over onto her side in bed, facing the window, and at first I can't see her face as I carry the tray over to the bedside table and set it down next to the piles of used paper tissues. She's still coughing, of course, but the bucket looks as if it hasn't been used.

"I brought you some soup," I say, my voice sounding extremely muffled thanks to the gas mask.

Slowly, she rolls over to look at me. It's shocking to see how drained and ill she looks, and her skin has turned almost yellow, while her eyes are bloodshot. She also seems to have lost weight, even though it's been less than a day since I last saw her. All in all, she's doing a damn good impression of someone who's getting dangerously sick, and right now it looks like it might even be touch and go whether she makes it through another night.

"Thank you," she rasps, barely able to get the words out. Her throat sounds so dry, as if she's swallowed razor blades and bramble.

"I'll come up for the tray in about an hour," I tell her. "See if you can eat something. It's probably good for you. It's home-made, so it's fresh and..." My voice trails off as I realize how weird I must sound. It's ridiculous, trying to have a normal conversation from under a gas mask.

"What are you wearing?" she asks weakly, narrowing her eyes as she stares at me. She starts looking around the room, as if panicked by my appearance. "Where the hell am I?"

"You're in our house," I say. "This is just a precaution. I don't want to get whatever you've got".

She stares at me for a moment, before breaking down into another coughing fit. I stand and watch, but eventually I realize that she's probably not going to stop any time soon. Just as I'm about to turn and leave the room, I spot something on her hands, and I see that she's coughing up blood. Not a lot of blood, but definitely a small amount, spraying against her fingers. I walk around the bed and see that there's more blood down on the other side, splattered against the wall and the floor.

"Holy shit," I mutter quietly. My heart starts racing as I realize that this is absolute, final proof that whatever's affecting Lydia, it's far more serious than simply flu. Leaning closer, I see that some of the blood is actually a kind of fleshy material. It's almost as if she's starting to literally cough up part of her lungs or throat.

"I'm okay," she splutters, before starting to cough again. This time, I spot a larger piece of flesh coming out, as if part of the lining of her throat has become detached. She wipes it on the bedsheets, almost as if she's not even aware of its existence. "I'm fine," she says breathlessly.

"You need to see if you can keep the soup down," I say, even though I know it must be a forlorn hope. To be honest, I'm starting to wonder if there's any way she can even survive. Unless she starts improving soon, she's going to end up losing too much blood and too many liquids. "You... You should just try to relax".

"Can you -" she starts to say, before she starts coughing again. "Can you call a doctor? I think I might need to see someone".

"The phones aren't working," I say.

"Still?" I can see the panic in her eyes, as if she's starting to realize that the situation is pretty hopeless. "What the fuck's wrong with this place?

Why can't you have fucking phones that work?"

"It's not that," I reply. "It's all over the place. The power's out".

"Fucking hicks," she says, spitting up another blob of blood. "It's like I've wondered into one of those horror films where a bunch of country idiots take someone hostage".

"We're trying to help you," I insist. "All the power's been off for a day now. Someone's gonna fix it, though, and then we'll get someone here straight away". I turn to leave the room, but suddenly she grabs my arm and pulls me back.

"Don't leave me here," she says, staring at me. "Get me outside. I need to be outside".

"No-one's gonna leave you here," I say. For the first time, I get a really good, close-up view of her face. It's shocking to see how far she's deteriorated. Her skin seems to have become slightly yellow, and a little translucent, while her lips are chapped and cracked, and there's dried blood in her nostrils. Her eyes are bloodshot, and she seems to be sweating heavily.

"I don't -" she starts to say, before she suddenly starts coughing again. This time, although she tries to cover her mouth, some of the blood sprays against the gas mask. I pull away and step back toward the door, shocked at the mixture of blood and phlegm that's covering the eyepiece. Instinctively, I try to wipe it away, although then I realize that I'm getting the mess on my bare hands.

"Shit," I mutter.

"I'm sorry -" she says breathlessly.

"It's okay," I say, staring at my hand and imagining the germs spreading like wildfire.

"No," she gasps, trying to get out of bed. "It's not okay".

"Stay there!" I shout. "You can't leave the room!"

"You can't keep me here," she says, stumbling as she tries to reach me. She's clearly pretty weak, and now that she's up, I can see that there's blood on her legs and feet. "It's better if I just leave. I'm only going to make you all worse".

"You can't come out here!" I say, stepping back through the door. "You need to stay in bed!" I wait for a moment, but she's still making her way toward me. Finally, figuring I've got no other options, I pull the door shut and hold the handle tightly as Lydia tries to get out.

"Let me out!" she shouts. "I can't be in here!"

"You have to!" I shout back.

"Let me out right now!" she screams. "I'm not joking! If you don't let me out, I'll have you arrested for imprisonment!" She starts coughing again. "Let me out!" she rasps, and it sounds as if she's sliding down onto the floor.

"I can't," I say quietly, although I doubt she

can hear me through the gas mask and the door.

After a moment, I hear her stumbling or crawling away from the door, and finally she seems to have got back onto the bed. She's coughing again, but this time there's another noise mixed in: I think she's sobbing. I keep my hand firmly on the door handle, not even pausing to wipe the mess from my mask. Listening to the sound of the bed creaking as she gets back under the covers, I quickly go to the cabinet at the top of the stairs and sort through the drawers until I find the key-chain. Luckily, the first one I try turns out to be the right one for the door to the guest room, and I take a step back once the door is locked. If I hadn't been wearing the gas mask, I'd have got a full load of blood and snot straight in my face.

"Sorry," I say quietly.

Hurrying through to the bathroom, I remove my shirt and trousers, and finally I slip out of the gas mask and drop it into the bath before I start washing my hands. Unfortunately, after just a few seconds the water flows to a trickle, and I'm forced to grab some anti-bacterial gel from the cabinet and slather it all over my hands and arms. It takes about ten minutes before I decide that I might finally be clean, and then I use some more of the gel on the gas mask, trying to make sure it's as clear as possible. By the time I'm done, most of the gel is used up, but I figure I had no choice. At least this way, I know I've managed to get all the germs off my body.

"Is she okay?" my mother asks. I turn to see her standing in the doorway, looking worried. She must have heard Lydia shouting for me to let her out.

"She coughed blood on me," I say. "By accident, but... I managed to get it off, though. I'm clean".

"It sounded like she was trying to get out of the room".

"She was," I say. At that moment, we both hear the sound of Lydia trying to open the door again. "I locked it," I explain. "It seemed like it'd be better to keep it contained in that room, rather than letting her wander through the house".

"That's probably a good idea," she replies. "Where's the key?"

I reach into my pocket and hold it out to her.

"Keep it safe," she replies, before turning and walking away.

Taking a deep breath, I throw my old shirt and trousers into the laundry basket before going through to my room and find something fresh to wear. Once I'm done, I sit on the end of my bed and listen to the sound of Lydia still trying to get the door open. She starts calling out for someone to help her, but I know there's nothing we can do. We just need to wait until things get back to normal, and hope that by then there's still a chance to save her. I look up at the bulb that hangs from the ceiling. Any second now, it could flick back on and this whole nightmare could be over; I continue to stare at the bulb, hoping and praying that things are gonna get back to normal, convinced that the light might come back at any moment.

# ELIZABETH

*Manhattan*

"LET ME LAY IT out straight," Bob says, sitting at his desk in the office while he addresses the five of us who have gathered for this impromptu meeting. "We don't know what's happened. All we know is what we can see when we look out the window, and I think we've all seen the same things. Planes coming down, deserted streets, stationary traffic in the distance. These are not *good* things. It's very clear that there's been some kind of catastrophic event that has cut power and water to the city. The lack of intervention by any external agencies makes it pretty clear that this catastrophic event is not confined to New York. I think we're talking about something on a national level, possibly even international. Every hour that passes without some kind of sign from the outside world, things look worse and worse". He pauses for a moment. "If nobody's coming to the rescue, that can only mean one thing. There's nobody *left* to come to the rescue".

"I have a ham radio," says one of the other men, sitting over by the door. "I managed to run it from a reserve battery for a few minutes, but I didn't pick up any signals. I'm gonna try again this evening, if I can get a crank battery up and running. Maybe there's other people broadcasting out there".

"Did you try the emergency frequencies?" Bob asks.

The man nods. "Nothing's transmitting. The only thing I found was some of the old number stations. They're still going, but maybe there'll be something later".

"Keep an eye on it, Albert," Bob says. "We need to know as much as possible. No detail is too small".

"So no-one knows what's happened?" I continue, turning to look at the other man who's in the room. Wearing a scruffy business suit and with his feet up on a table, the man looks kind of bored by the whole thing.

"No-one knows," Bob replies. "Whatever it is, though, it's serious. I don't think we can expect it to be fixed too soon. I'm not saying it's impossible, but we need to plan for the medium-term at the very least".

"But there are systems in place," I say. "They have emergency measures for this type of thing". I wait for someone to back me up. "Right?" I say, turning to the others. "Things can't just stop!" "There are various counter-emergency programs in place," the radio guy says. "They're designed to swing into action as soon as something like this happens. The thing is, they *haven't* swung into action, which suggests they're not going to. Whatever's happened, it seems to have caught everyone by surprise".

"Is it nuclear?" Henry asks. I can see the fear in his eyes, and I'm making sure to keep a close eye on him. He seems to be getting more and more fidgety.

"If it was nuclear, we'd know already," the radio guy says. "Nuclear isn't discriminating. There'd be widespread radiation poisoning, and atmospheric disturbances, and we'd probably have felt the ground shake. Plus, you know, the whole mushroom thing. This incident, whatever it is, seems to have knocked out a hell of a lot of people, but it's left some of us standing. That's not nuclear. I'm thinking it might be more biological in nature".

"Although," Bob says, interrupting, "I *do* want to raise a point about safety at the various reactors. I remember watching the news a while back, when that Japanese facility was damaged by the tsunami. Those places can last a few days without cooling, but after that, things can get dicey. If there's anything that concerns me in the medium-term, it's the possibility of something going wrong at one of our facilities and potentially causing a disaster. I think there's a real chance of the situation deteriorating rapidly over the next few days and, again, we need to be prepared".

"There's something else we haven't discussed," the radio guy adds, "which is the lack of people on the streets. I walked to the end of the block this morning, just to take a look. I didn't meet anyone else. Obviously it's highly unlikely that we're the only ones who are alive, but I think it's reasonable to assume that the vast majority of people are staying inside. They're scared. There's also the possibility that at least some of those people are dead. Again, if this was some kind of biological event, it might have taken a while for symptoms to manifest, by which point a majority of the population would be infected. If the onset of those symptoms was then rapid, there might not have been any time for the warning to spread".

"We saw a body," I say. "We were on the roof, and we saw a body in a window in one of the buildings opposite. I couldn't be sure, but he looked wrong, somehow".

"There's a body in the lobby of the hotel

nearby," the radio guy continues. "He didn't look good, either. Kind of the wrong color. His skin was yellowy-gray. Got me wondering whether we're dealing with some kind of outbreak. I think that's what we need to be assuming at this point in time".

"It's possible," Bob replies, "but again, we have to wonder why we seem to have been spared. Perhaps it's just a coincidence, but judging from my observations of the landscape so far, it seems this building has enjoyed a substantially higher survival rate than many others. In fact, as far as I can tell, there are very few survivors in New York at this particular moment".

"There's a lot of dead bodies in cars," says the radio guy. "A *lot*".

"But not everyone's dead," Henry says, turning to me. "Some people have survived. We've survived, so other people have survived". There's a hint of desperation in his voice, and I understand why: he's worried about our parents, since they were most likely out at the airport or a little way along the freeway when this disaster struck. The weird thing is, they're probably only a few miles away, but suddenly 'a few miles' seems like a huge distance.

"It can't just be us," I tell Henry. "There's no way we'd be the only ones who've survived. That just wouldn't make sense".

Henry pauses for a moment, before turning

back to look at Bob. "What about our food?" he asks, a clear hint of anger in his voice. "You came and took our food. *Our* food. Our parents bought that food, and they left it for us. And the water. We want it all back".

"Calm down," I say, reaching out and grabbing his arm.

"I'll calm down when they give our food back," he replies, pulling away. "We don't know how long this things gonna be happening, so we need our food".

"And you can have it," Bob replies. "If that's what you want, feel free. As I said before, I'll even help you carry it back up to your apartment and stick it straight back where we found it. But hear me out first. When we came and took the food from your refrigerator, it was genuinely because we thought the pair of you had skipped out of here. That was a mistake. Now that we have the food in our central area, however, I'm proposing that we pool our resources. With all due respect to you and your sister, you're kids. You don't know how to ration yourselves and how to control yourselves, so maybe it'd be better all round if we work together. If you're willing to share some of your food, we can do other things for you".

"There's nothing we want," Henry says, "except our food and water".

"What about heat?" Bob pauses for a

moment. "I can heat some water and fill bottles for you. Keep you warm at night. And water? I have several sanitation barrels that'll at least allow you to flush your toilet. Now, I have no motivation to share these things with you, if you don't share what you've got with me. That's why I'm proposing that we pool together and work as a team. There are six of us in this building, including Mrs DeWitt, and I think we can easily stretch things out to last a week or two. By then, with God's grace, some semblance of order will have been restored".

"We don't want any of your shit," Henry replies. "Give us our food and water". "It's okay, son," Bob continues. "You're scared. I understand that -"

"I'm not scared!" Henry shouts back at him, reaching into his pocket to grab the handle of his knife.

"You're not?" Bob shrugs. "That's pretty unusual. I'm scared. I'm scared that the military *won't* come and restore order. I'm scared that it'll turn out that there's some kind of virus causing all these deaths. I'm scared that no matter what we do, we'll run out of everything and then we'll be stuck here. If you're not scared of these things, son, then I suppose the only reason must be that you know something the rest of us don't. So, please, enlighten us. Just what is it that prevents you from being scared right now?" He pauses. "Is it that knife in your pocket? Is that what it is?"

Henry doesn't reply; he just stands there, looking as if he could be about to do something very stupid.

"Aren't we over-reacting?" I say, trying to calm things down. "It's been a day. That's all. A day's not very long. That's just twenty-four hours. They might still come and help us, right?" I turn to the others. "Right?"

"We can't assume that," Bob says. "Only a fool sits and waits for others to save his skin".

"But they wouldn't just stop being there," I continue. "Maybe it's taking them a little longer than they thought to get ready, but they could still turn up at any moment".

"And who are 'they', exactly?" Bob asks.

"The government. The military". I stare at him. "We can't give up yet. We've got to stay optimistic".

"Tell that to your brother," Bob replies. "He's the one holding the knife. I'm just trying to create a safe environment for all of us, so we can get through this as best we can. We can give your food back. We don't *need* it, though it'd make things a hell of a lot easier. But we can get by without it, and you two can go merrily back up to your apartment. Or just one of you can go. You can split the food, and one of you can choose to stick with us, and the other can go off on his own. It's up to you. I'm not telling you what you should do; I'm just laying out another option for you".

"We want out food," Henry says, carefully taking the knife out of his pocket. "We can handle everything else just fine".

"Is that right?" Smiling, Bob opens a drawer in his desk and takes out a small handgun.

"Let's go," I say, standing up and grabbing Henry's arm. "Let's go!" I say again, starting to get worried. I really don't like guns, and I have no idea whether we can trust this Bob guy. For all I know, he might decide to shoot us both, purely so he can keep his haul from our apartment.

"Calm down," Bob says, placing the gun on the desk. "It's loaded, but I'm not gonna use it. I just wanted you to see that, in the grand scheme of things, a fucking carving knife isn't the be-all and end-all of the situation. It's fine. We'll bring your food back up, all of it. It's currently sitting in a refrigerator in the basement, hooked up to a generator, but we'll haul it all up to your place for you. You'll have it back within the hour".

"And the water," Henry says.

"And the water".

"All of it!"

"All of it".

"Okay," Henry mutters, before turning and storming out of the room.

"Your brother's pretty scared," Bob says,

looking over at me.

"Our parents are missing," I reply.

"A lot of people are missing. I doubt there's anyone in this room who isn't worried about someone else. This is the kind of situation that tests a man and makes him show his true mettle, though. A real man stays calm and comes up with a plan, rather than panicking and waving knives around. I hope your brother can keep himself together. If he can't, I'm not going to stand for any Bad behavior".

"He'll be fine," I say, realizing that Bob just issued a thinly-veiled threat.

"I'm sure he will," Bob replies, placing the gun back in the drawer. "If you change your mind, though, you know where to find us. If there's a significant change in the situation, or if we learn anything else, then I can assure you that as a courtesy I'll be happy to let you know. Otherwise, any favors or resources you might want, you can negotiate with us on a day-by-day basis. I'm sure we'll be able to come to some kind of arrangement". He stares at me for a moment, and slowly a grin begins to spread across his lips. "I'm sure you've got some skills or abilities you could trade," he adds eventually.

Over by the wall, the radio guy lets out a chuckle.

"I'm fine with my brother, thanks," I say, shivering at the thought of how these sleazy assholes are looking at me. "We're just going to wait it out up there". Walking over to the door, I pause for a moment and look back at him. "How much longer do you think this is going to last?" I ask. "I mean, honestly, on a gut level, you must have some idea of how bad it's looking". I wait for him to answer. "A day? A week?"

He sighs. "I think it's starting to look very bad indeed," he says eventually. "I hold out hope that thing are gonna get better at some point, but whatever's happened, it's far greater than anyone could have anticipated. I'd caution you to accept that we're currently living in an essentially lawless society. The ones who can enforce the rules are the ones who can make them. You need to find a way to simmer your brother down. You got that?"

I nod, before making my way out of the room and back through to the stairwell. I can hear Henry several floors up, heading to our apartment. To be honest, I can't help feeling that we might be making a mistake by failing to work with the others. After all, they seem to know a lot more about the situation, and they seem to have things like generators and at least some kind of understanding of what's happening. I don't like the idea of Henry and me sitting up there in our apartment, shivering and trying to make do with the food that we've got, while the rest of the building gets on with some kind of group plan. Still, I can't leave Henry up there alone, so right now I have to stick with him. Most likely, everything'll be fixed within a day or two anyway; but if this thing drags on much longer, I'm going to have to find a way to persuade Henry to reconsider. I just hope things get back to normal before it's too late.

# DAY 3

# THOMAS

*Oklahoma*

"ANYTHING?"

My mother looks up from the kitchen table, where she's writing something in her old notebook. "No," she says after a moment. "Not yet".

Walking over to the sink, I turn the cold tap and wait to see if any water comes out. I know it's a forlorn hope, but I perform this ritual a couple of times each day. My reasoning is that at some point, things have to start getting back to normal. The water *has* to start running and the lights *have* to come back on, and then we can begin the recovery process. Just because there's nothing yet, it doesn't necessarily follow that we're screwed forever. They won't let us just die out here. They won't let everything fall apart like this. They're working on put things right. I know they are. Whoever 'they' are...

"I had a sudden idea in the night," my mother says, still writing. "It occurred to me that maybe we should keep a diary of what happens, so we can refer back to it when this is all over". She adds a couple more lines to the book, before setting her pen aside and sitting back with a satisfied smile. "Do you remember when I used to write bedtime stories for you, and for Joseph? I don't know why I ever gave that up. This seems like the perfect time to freshen up some old habits".

I watch as she adds some more lines to her notebook. There's something slightly pathetic about the sight of her reverting to an activity she abandoned more than a decade ago. It's almost as if her fear of the future is forcing her into the past.

"What are you writing?" I ask eventually.

"Just in idea I had when I was trying to get to sleep. I had to wait until morning, of course, so I could see to write. I could barely close my eyes, of course. I was too excited, and..." She pauses, and the smile fades from her lips. "Well, I'm not really sure why I bothered now. It seems silly. But you never know. It might be useful".

"Sure," I say quietly. Even though I don't really understand her point, I figure I might as well let her get on with whatever makes her feel better.

Walking over to the fridge, which is still a little cooler than the rest of the house, I open the door and grab a bottle of water. We were pretty well-stocked when this began, but we're starting to run low and I doubt we've got enough for much more than another day. Suddenly, even the smallest things are cause for concern.

"Try not to drink too much," my mother says.

"I'm going to put out some butts," I reply. "Dad's got some big barrels in the barn. I figured it might rain, so we could collect the water".

"You're not allowed to collect rain-water," she says firmly.

"What?"

"It's against the law. You're not allowed to do it. You can get fined. It's part of the local land management rules".

"Who's gonna stop us?" I ask.

"Thomas, it's against the law!"

I stare at her for a moment. "I think I'll do it anyway," I say eventually. "Just to be safe". Looking up at the ceiling, I listen out for any sign of Lydia coughing in the guest room. I could hear her for most of the night, but she stopped a couple of hours ago and now the silence, which was so welcome at first, seems ominous. It's hard to believe that she's suddenly recovered

"I have no idea," my mother says suddenly.

"About what?"

"About her". She follows my gaze up to the ceiling. "I have no idea how she is. I don't think we should open the door, though. Whatever she's got, I don't want it infecting the rest of us, even if it's just a common cold. We've got enough to deal with, without having to get sick at the same time".

"We can't just leave her in there forever," I say. "What if she's dying?" I wait for her to respond, but she seems to be deliberately avoiding eye contact. "We can't just forget about her!" I say eventually.

She looks down at her notebook, clearly unable to answer the question.

"Do you think there's some kind of sickness?" I ask.

"What do you mean?"

I pause, reluctant to give voice to the ideas that have been going around and around in my head for the past twenty-four hours. "Do you think something's happened?" I say eventually. "Like, a virus or something. I mean, everything seems to have stopped, and then Lydia turns up with this illness, and it seems like it can't just be a coincidence. The fire's still burning from that plane that came down. Why wouldn't they come and see what's happened?"

She shakes her head. "You're being melodramatic. You've seen too many disaster films".

"So you think it's all just a coincidence?"

"I think we'll have to wait and see," she replies firmly, clearly trying to convince herself that everything's going to be okay. "When the internet and the television are back up and running, we'll find out the truth. It's obviously something big, but I don't want us jumping to conclusions. There's probably a perfectly reasonable explanation -"

"Like a virus," I say, interrupting her.

"No!" she replies, sounding a little exasperated. "Why would there be a virus? Where would it come from?"

"Asia. Some kind of flu, or maybe something that escaped from a lab somewhere, or an attack -"

"What are you *talking* about, Thomas?" She stares at me as if I'm insane; as if I've wandered in and started suggesting the most insane ideas in the entire world. "This isn't a film," she continues. "This is real life, not some kind of paranoid fantasy world. Obviously *something* has happened that has caused a degree of disruption, but it's by no means the end of the world. We have enough to deal with, waiting for everything to get sorted out, without you coming through and spouting off with these absurd ideas. If you don't have anything constructive to say, please don't say anything at all. We need to just stay calm and get on with our daily lives as usual".

"Where's Dad?" I ask after a moment.

"Your father's on his way back from Scottsville".

"How do you know?"

"Because that's what he said he'd be doing this morning!"

"But you don't *know*," I reply. "You hope he's coming back, but you don't know for certain".

Sighing, she gets up and walks over to the sink, where she starts wiping a couple of dirty plates with a dry sponge. It seems like a futile kind of gesture, as if she's just doing the things that make her feel better. "You might feel compelled to assume the worst," she says after a moment, "but the rest of us have things to be doing. The world isn't going to stop just so you can talk about disasters. Whatever's happened, it's bad, but it's not as bad as you're trying to make out. Frankly, I wonder about your state of mind, since you seem so determined to cause trouble and make everyone panic. Do you want something bad to happen?" She pauses for a moment. "Your father isn't due back until the early afternoon. It takes time to travel back from Scottsville, you know. He can't just fly here in a couple of minutes".

"He said he wouldn't be late," I point out. "He promised -"

"Are you done here?" she snaps, turning to me with a look of real frustration in her eyes. "Are you planning to spend the whole morning just picking holes in everything and causing trouble? Is that really the best thing you can think to be doing right now? Or do you want to do something constructive like tidying the yard or bringing some wood in from the shed? We still have to attend to our normal lives, Thomas, in-between these fanciful ideas about the end of the world. Even if you can't stop yourself from thinking these things, I'd be grateful if you could keep from saying them out loud. We're all trying to get along as best we can. If you really want to be useful, you can go and find your brother. Tell him this is hardly the time to go wandering off".

I stare at her, trying to work out if there's any way I can get her to see the truth. She seems to be sticking her head in the sand and just hoping that things work out. My mother's usually such a calm and quiet person, so this sudden display of anger is clearly a sign that she's worried.

"I'd appreciate some help," she continues after a moment, before returning to her notebook. "Your father's taken off to Scottsville for *however* long, and your brother's no use. I'd really be grateful if you could at least stay on my side for a while, Thomas. A little help would go a very long way right now".

Realizing that there's no point arguing with her, I turn and head back through to the hallway and up the stairs. Just as I'm about to go to my room, I stop and look over at the door to the guest room. The lack of any kind of noise is starting to worry me, since Lydia has spent most of the past twenty-four hours coughing her guts up and now she's stopped completely. It could be a trap, of course; she knows that we've locked the door, and she might be hoping to lure one of us inside so she can escape. In fact, she might have recovered completely. Then again, I can't shake the feeling that Lydia's illness is a sign of something darker and more dangerous. As I put my ear to the door, I decide that if there's no development by midday, I'll go in and check on her. I can't just ignore the fact that she's here, and hope that she'll suddenly pull through. I pause for a moment, hoping against hope that there'll be some signs of life from the other side of the door, but all I hear is silence.

"Lydia?" I say.

Nothing.

"Lydia?"

Still nothing.

I don't want to believe the worst, but I saw how sick she was yesterday. If something bad *has* happened to her, it means there's a much more serious situation in the world in general. I keep telling myself that the idea of a virus is too over-the-top and too melodramatic, but at the same time it's starting more and more to seem like the only explanation that actually fits. And if there *is* a virus on the loose, it's starting to look as if Lydia has brought it straight into our house.

# ELIZABETH

*Manhattan*

I'VE BEEN AWAKE FOR a few hours, but I haven't moved. A cold wind is howling through the apartment, but I'm warm under a pile of old duvets. If I concentrate really hard, I can trick myself into thinking that everything's okay. My mother's in the kitchen making breakfast, and my father's getting ready to go to work, and my brother's watching some crappy cartoon on his laptop. It's just an ordinary day, full of all the annoyances that bug me every day. I might try to phone Carla later, or go for a wander through the streets of Manhattan, or get a smoothie in a cafe, or...

It's no use.

I can't keep it up.

I know I can't do any of these things.

For one thing, my parents have been missing for two days now, caught up in whatever natural disaster has struck the city. For another, the phone network is down so I can't phone Carla, and going for a wander through the streets of Manhattan would be far too dangerous. All I can do is stay right here and wait for everything to go back to normal. It could still happen. The lights could come on, and my parents could come home, and the city could come back to life. The alternative is too horrible to contemplate, because the longer this whole thing lasts, the less likely it becomes that things will get back to normal soon. Or ever. In fact, staring at the ceiling on the morning of the third day, I force myself to contemplate for the first time the possibility that this won't ever end. What if this is how things are going to be forever? What if the old world - with people and cars and phones and internet and planes and all those things - is gone for good?

Forcing myself to get a grip, I remind myself that it's not going to be like that *at all*. It might take a few more days or weeks, but things are going to get back to normal eventually. Our parents *will* be back and the power *will* come back on. It's so tempting to assume the worst, and to give up, but things are going to get better. We just need to have some faith. And until then, I'm in charge. When our parents went away for a few days, they told me to keep an eye on Henry. The situation has changed, of course, but basically I'm still going to have to 'keep an eye' on him. If anything bad happens, it's my fault. I'm the older one, so I have to look after us both. Until this is over, the responsibility for keeping us safe is all mine.

Sitting up, I take a deep breath and tell myself that I can't just stay in bed all day. Although it's tempting to just wait for someone to come and fix things, I know that I need to deal with situation; I need to make sure Henry's okay, and I need to work out what we're going to eat and drink today. In fact, now that it's looking like we're in this for the long-haul, I guess it might be time to start making proper plans. With the duvets wrapped around my body, I shuffle across the room and open the door. The force of the ice-cold wind hits me immediately, almost blowing me back to my bed; as well as the wind blowing through the apartment, there's a surprisingly thick cloud of small black particles blowing along from somewhere else in the house. Our apartment has always been so perfectly sealed off from the rest of the world, like a small isolated box perched high up on top of the building, that it seems really strange to now have the natural world invading the space. It's as if we've lost some kind of battle, and it's tempting to think that now the wind and cold has got inside, we'll never get it back out again.

Forcing my way to the front room, I see that our DIY attempt to fix the broken window has come loose, and there's a new, fine layer of dust and black little particles all over the floor. There's a smattering of rain in the air, and the sky outside looks gray and threatening. The ash-like black particles, swirling in the air around me, most likely come from the wreckage of the plane that crashed a few blocks away, and which is still burning after more than a day. The fire is pushing charred wreckage and dust up into the air, spreading its fine mist far and wide before everything starts raining down again. All these tiny little black pieces, burned to a crisp; it's hard to believe they were once part of a plane. Well, maybe they weren't part of the plane; maybe they were part of the luggage, or the passengers. Reaching out, I move my hand slowly through the particles; they're so fine and delicate, I can barely feel them as they disintegrate against my skin. A shiver passes through my body and I step back from the window.

"Henry!" I call out, though I doubt my brother will be able to hear me over the noise of the wind. I head through to the kitchen, but there's no sign of him. Grabbing one of our few remaining bottles of water, I take a sip and stare at the food in our fridge. It's not much, but the situation could be worse: at least we have a load of cheese and bread, and basic stuff like butter and mayonnaise. The fridge isn't working, of course, but the apartment's cold enough to keep everything cool. Walking over to the cupboards, I find that we've got plenty of tins of beans and spaghetti. It's not the best food in the world, but it's something. At a conservative estimate, we can easily last for a couple of weeks, and that's without even bothering to cut down on our consumption. If we plan properly, and eliminate waste, I'm pretty sure we can keep going for at least a month. The thought of a month of living like this, though, sends a shiver through my body. It's just not possible. We can't be like this forever.

"Henry!" I call out again. Part of me wants him to get up and help me, but another part of me is kind of glad that he's managing to sleep. Shuffling over to the far side of the kitchen, still wrapped in the duvets, I look down at our bottles of water. While we've got plenty of food, water is more of a concern. When this thing started, we had a dozen large bottles of mineral water and some cola; we've now drunk all the cola, and we're down to eight bottles of water. There's also some beer and wine in one of the cupboards, which I suppose counts as liquids. Still, we're gonna run dry much sooner than we starve, but I figure we can maybe collect rain water up on the roof. As long as we plan things in advance, it can't be too hard to find water.

As I make my way back through to the front

room, I realize that in some ways things don't look too bad. We have food and water, and we're not in any immediate danger. In fact, the biggest problem might be the temperature. With an icy wind blowing through the broken window, the temperate in the apartment is gone way down to zero or maybe even further. There's also the question of this little black particles in the air; although they look kind of pretty blowing through the white, dust-colored apartment, I'm not entirely sure that it's safe to be breathing this stuff into our lungs. We need to fix the window, and we need to do it properly this time, but I'm pretty sure we don't have anything suitable; I guess we'll have to go down to the basement and look in our parents' storage area. What we need is some kind of large piece of wood, or at least *something* that's solid enough to withstand the force of the wind.

"Henry?" I call out, turning and wandering back across the front room. "Henry!" Making my way along the corridor, I stop outside his bedroom and knock loudly. "You need to get up," I call out. "I want to go up onto the roof and see if we can get some rainwater, and then we need to go to the basement and look for some stuff". I pause, waiting for him to groan or yell at me to leave him alone. "Henry," I continue, knocking again, "can you get up?"

Nothing.

"Okay," I say, "I'm gonna count to three and

then I'm gonna come in. Fair warning. One. Two". I leave a little pause. "Three," I add eventually, before opening the door.

He's not there.

Stepping over to his bed, I see that the duvets have been pushed aside but Henry himself is nowhere to be found. I reach down and feel the bedsheets; they're cold, which suggests he's not been here for a while. Hurrying through to the bathroom, I double-check that there's no sign of him, and that's when the panic really sets in: I've repeatedly told Henry that we need to stay here and wait for help, but he's been arguing for us to go out and see what's happening. Is it possible that he decided to take matters into his own hand and just go out into the city? Running back through to my bedroom, I throw the duvets onto the bed before heading back to the front door. I slept in my clothes, so at least it doesn't take me too long to slip my shoes on and run out into the hallway. Wherever Henry's gone, I need to get to him before he blunders into danger. With no phones and no email, though, I have no way of tracking him down. If something happens to him while he's out of the building, I'll never be able to forgive myself.

# THOMAS

*Oklahoma*

IT TAKES ME A while to find Joe, since he's not in any of the usual places. By 'usual places', I mean the dirt patch behind the barn and the broken chicken coop over the crest of the hill. Usually, when he wants to hide away and not be found for a while, Joe goes to one of these places, but to my surprise he seems to have found somewhere else to go this time. I spend most of the morning wandering around the farm, looking into every nook and cranny that could conceivably give my brother some cover, and after a while I start to worry that maybe he's gone further than usual. Finally, however, I reach the old milking station and spot two legs sticking around from around the back.

"Lydia's sick," I say, walking over to him. "She's -" As soon as I get around the corner, I see that Joe's sitting with his back to the wall, sipping from a half-empty bottle of whiskey. I stare at him for a moment. "Are you drunk?" I ask eventually.

He turns to me, and it's clear that he can barely even focus properly.

"You're drunk," I say.

"And you're ugly," he replies. "At least I'll sober up eventually".

Stepping over to him, I grab the bottle and toss it away. It doesn't break when it hits the dirt, but the last of the whiskey dribbles away.

"What the *fuck*?" he says, staring at me with white-hot anger. He tries to get up, but the effort is clearly too much and he slumps back down. "Did you just do what I think you did, you little dick?"

"You're drunk," I say again. "Of all the days, why the hell do you have to be drunk right now?"

"I believe this is a free country -" he starts to reply.

"Do you have any idea what's going on?" I shout. "Mom's going nuts at the kitchen table, and your precious new girlfriend's sick in the guest room!"

"Is that right?" he asks. "Well, I guess there's not much for me to be doing. Be a good kid and fetch me another bottle of whiskey, yeah?"

"Dad's not back yet," I say.

"So what?"

"He should be back right about now," I continue, "but there's no sign of him. He knows it's important to keep to time. If he's not back, it means something's wrong".

"Or he got drunk last night and he's sleeping it off in a ditch".

"He didn't get drunk," I reply. "You know that and I know that. Dad's not an irresponsible asshole. He would've set out to come back from Scottsville this morning at first light, and he'd have been back by now".

"So he got a puncture," Joe says. "Big deal. He's got a spare, but it'll take him a while to get it changed. He's probably cursing by the side of the road right now, popping out another hernia as he tries to jack the damn truck up. Serves him right. He'll get it sorted in the end, but he'll be in a foul mood when he gets back". He stares at me. "What? What's your explanation? You think a fucking jet plane fell on his head?"

"I think something's wrong at Scottsville," I say. "Maybe other places too".

"Yeah?" He smiles. "And what are you gonna do about it? Grab a red cape and fly to the rescue?"

"Lydia's *really* sick," I say, hoping to make him realize that we can't just sit around and wait for something to happen. "She was coughing her guts up all night, and then a few hours ago she just stopped".

"And? Did you go in and check on her?"

I shake my head.

"Why the hell not?"

"We had to lock her in the guest room".

"You did what?" Scrabbling to his feet, he steps toward me and pushes me back. "You locked her away? What the hell did you do that for?"

"There's something wrong with her," I say, my heart racing.

"There's something wrong with *you*!" he shouts, pushing me again. "You can't go around locking people up just 'cause they're sick!" He stumbles toward me again, but this time I get out of his way. He's clearly wasted, and he can barely even stay upright. Steadying himself against a tree, he pauses for a moment. "Fuck," he mutters. "She's gonna think we're a bunch of fucking hillbillies. Do you have any idea how fucking dumb you are?"

"Mom agreed," I say.

"And you listened to that dumb bitch?" Suddenly he lurches toward me, swinging his fist at my face. I step back and he trips on a root, landing hard on the dirt. He immediately gets back up and turns to face me. "You know what you're gonna do?" he says, barely able to focus on me. "You're gonna go right back to the house, and you're gonna unlock the door and you're gonna go in and apologize to her. And then you're gonna make her some breakfast and then you're gonna pray to God that she doesn't call the cops and tell 'em you and that mad bitch kept her prisoner overnight, and then I'm gonna come and take her away, and neither of us is ever gonna come back to this pig-fucking shit-hole of a farm again. Do you understand?" He stares at me, swaying slightly as he tries to stay on his feet. "Do you understand?" he screams, his face turning red with anger.

"You're drunk," I say quietly.

Once again, he lurches at me. This time, I'm not quite able to get out of the way in time, and he manages to grab my arm and pull me down to the ground. Climbing on top of me, he jams his elbow into my throat before smashing his knee into my belly. The pain is intense, and for a moment I can't even breathe. Struggling to get him off me, I try kneeing him in the ass, but I can't quite reach. Instead, I grab his shoulders and try to push him away.

"Listen to me, pig-fucker," he says firmly. "You're right. I'm fucked. But even when I'm fucked, I'm ten times the man you are, and I'm ten times smarter and more useful than that bitch we call Mom. So you're gonna listen to me, or I swear to God I'll break your fucking neck. Do you understand?" He leans closer, staring straight into my eyes, and then - as if to prove his point - he grinds his elbow deeper into my neck, making it hard for me to breathe. "I asked you a question," he says after a moment. "Do you understand what I'm telling you?"

Refusing to give in, I stare back at him.

"You're pissing me off," he continues, his whiskey-soaked breath filling my nose. "Let me put this another way. What if you're right? What if the whole world's fucked, and Dad's not coming back from Scottsville? Who do you think's gonna be in charge around here? You? No way. It'll be me, and there's nothing you can do to stop that, so maybe you should start thinking about your loyalties. Got it?" After a moment, he crunches his elbow even harder against my neck, and now I can't breathe at all. I reach up to push him away, but he's too strong and I start to wonder if maybe in his drunken state he might be more dangerous than usual. "Got it?" he shouts.

"Yes!" I gasp, and he immediately lets go. As I catch my breath, he moves over to a nearby tree and sits staring at me.

"Consider this a warning," he says darkly. "You're a good kid, Thomas, but I don't want you mouthing off at me. Do you understand? It doesn't have to be like this. As long as you show me some respect, we can work together just fine, but if you piss me off, I'll run you out of this place so fast, you won't know what's hit you. And if you try anything,

I'll hit back at you twice as hard. Now why don't you go and get me some more whiskey, and then go and check on Lydia and tell her I'll be along in a while. Or even better, if she's feeling better, tell her to come out here and see me. I wouldn't mind some proper company".

Getting to my feet, I brush dirt from my shirt and trousers. There's a part of me that wants to grab Joe and bounce his head off the nearest tree. I'm pretty sure I could hurt him, but there's no point; he'd just come back at me, and the end result wouldn't be much better than the situation I'm in at the moment. Joe's tougher, stronger and meaner than I could ever hope to be, and I guess I'll just have to be more subtle. Besides, he's just acting out while our father's away. As soon as the truck comes back from Scottsville and our father's back at home, Joe'll start to sober up and act normal again. He's had little blips like this before, but he always comes around eventually.

"Fuck you," I say, turning and walking away.

"What did you say?" he calls after me.

I don't look back at him. I just keep walking, focusing on the house in the distance.

"You little piece of crap!" he shouts. "You don't fucking talk to me like that, okay?"

He can fuck off and die if he thinks I'm taking him a bottle of whiskey. The guy's wasted anyway, so the worst that can happen is that he'll pass out and sleep for most of the day, and then he'll have a hangover for at least twenty-four hours after that, so I figure Joe's out of the picture for a while. Hopefully, our father will be back before too long; as I reach the house, I glance around and realize that there's still no sign of the truck. Looking over at the horizon, I see nothing except for smoke from the plane crash still rising into the sky. Maybe Joe's right; maybe the truck blew a tire, and that's why it's not back yet. Still, as these coincidences keep piling up, I'm getting more and more worried about how things are gonna work out.

# ELIZABETH

*Manhattan*

"HAVE YOU SEEN MY BROTHER?" I ask, rushing into the office down in the foyer of the building. I assumed Bob would be down here, but instead I find that the only person is Albert Carling, the guy from the second floor. He's sitting behind the main desk, fiddling with the knobs on a small radio. Albert's the kind of slightly shifty-looking, slightly smelly guy you might pass in the elevator a hundred times without necessarily making eye contact. To be honest, I'd completely ignored him until all this stuff started to happen; suddenly, with his radio, he seems like one of the most important and useful people in the world.

"Your brother?" he says, looking up.

"Did you see him come down here?" I continue. "He's gone missing".

He shakes his head. "What about the others? Where's Bob?"

"Bob's out".

"Out? Out where?"

Albert sniffs, as if he's deeply unimpressed by my sense of panic. "Said he was going to walk around the block and see what's what. That was a couple of hours ago, so I guess he should be back soon. If he's coming back at all". As he speaks, the radio squeals into life and a semi-regular, hissing pattern starts to come over the speaker. "Hello?" Albert barks into the microphone. "Anyone there?"

"If my brother comes back," I say, "you have to tell him to wait in our apartment. Okay? Tell him to just stay put and wait for -"

"Hello?" Albert says again, apparently ignoring me. "This is New York. Is anyone out there? Over".

"If my brother comes back -" I start to say again.

"Is anyone there?" asks a crackly voice, coming directly from the speaker.

"Hang on," Albert says, putting the microphone aside and grabbing another, smaller device. "This is New York," he says. "Repeat, this is New York. Identify yourself. Over".

"Who's that?" I ask, my heart soaring at the

prospect that we might have found other people who are still alive out there.

"Wait!" Albert hisses at me.

There's a rumble of static for a moment. "This is Jerry," says the other voice eventually. "I'm in Danbury, Connecticut. Something strange is happening here. There's no power, no water, no kind of emergency system in place. A lot of people are dead. Do you guys have any idea what the hell's going on? Over".

"It's the same here," Albert replies. "I've used a hand-crank to get my radio working, but it won't last long. What are things like in Danbury? Over".

"Everything's dead," the other voice says. "Power. Water. Phone lines. Even the emergency radio frequencies are shut off. I don't know what's happened, but people are dying. There are a couple of bodies out in the street, and I think something crashed a few miles out of town. We've got no information. There's no police, no anything. What about you? Over".

"Negative on the information," Albert says. "Have you been in contact with anyone else? Anyone from the government? Over".

"I spoke briefly to a woman in Rhode Island," Jerry says. "Picked her up on a low frequency. She said there were some sick people up there too. Real sick. Apart from that, she didn't have any information. It's hard making contact. It almost seems as if something's running deliberate interference. You get hold of a signal for a while, and then something comes and pushes you off, like there's a jammer being used. Are there sick people in New York too? Have you seen any sign of a relief effort? We've got nothing here. Over".

"Negative on the sick people," Albert says, "and negative on the relief effort. The city seems to be deserted. There's just a handful of us here, but the streets are empty. We can see miles of cars in the distance, though. When you say that people are sick, what exactly do you mean? How sick are they? Over".

"It's like a kind of fever," Jerry continues. "Like flu, but it affects different people differently. Some develop it over a few days, but with others, it seems to cut them down almost right away. A few people, like me, haven't been affected so far, but I don't know how long that's gonna last. I've never seen anything like it. It's almost as if it just swept through Danbury in a couple of hours, killing everyone around. One minute everything was fine, the next minute it was as if people were just dropping like flies all over the place. It's like something out of the apocalypse. Is it the same in New York?" There's a pause, before he remembers to add the sign-off. "Over".

"I guess," Albert says, glancing at me. "It's

more like the place is empty. We don't really know where the people went, but we're assuming they're inside. They -" As he speaks, there's a loud bang and the front of the radio falls off, with smoke billowing from inside. Albert leaps out of his chair and stares in shock as a small fire breaks out, burning up the interior of the radio unit with alarming speed and quickly spreading to a small pile of papers.

"What happened?" I ask, backing away.

"I must have overloaded the crank," he replies, clearly panicking a little as the radio continues to burn. He stares blankly at the flames, as if he expects them to just die down of their own accord.

Grabbing a fire extinguisher from the other side of the room, I spray white foam over the whole desk, quickly killing the fire. The force of the extinguisher is more extreme than I ever imagined, and I struggle to keep it under control. By the time I'm done, there's a real mess and my heart is racing, but at least the fire's out.

"Did you hear what he said?" Albert continues after a moment. "He said there's people dead up in Connecticut. Dead in the streets. That's over a hundred miles away. This thing must be big. If it's spread as far as Connecticut, maybe it's gone across the whole country, maybe even the whole world".

"I heard," I reply, putting the empty fire extinguisher on the floor. For some strange reason, I feel totally calm, as if my body is refusing to let me fall apart. All I can think about is my brother, and my parents, and how we're going to make sure we get through this. "But just 'cause they've got it in Connecticut," I say after a moment, "and just 'cause it's here, that doesn't mean it's everywhere, does it? It can't have struck everyone. There'll be people in bunkers working to sort things out. Maybe it'll take them a few days, but they'll get their stuff together. There'll be helicopters or something arriving soon, with aid and some kind of vaccine".

"You don't know that," Albert replies.

"I do," I say. "I can feel it. It has to happen. Even if a lot of people have died, there'll still be enough to get things back to normal".

"And if there's not?" he asks. "What if there's some kind of virus that's killed everyone?"

"And they all got sick at the same time?" I ask. "Are you seriously suggesting that all of this is possible? There was nothing on the news about this. I didn't hear one person complain about being sick".

"Maybe there was a trigger," he continues. "Maybe people got infected over time, and the virus lay dormant until some kind of global event triggered its activation -"

"That doesn't even make sense," I reply, interrupting him.

"And then there's gonna be a second wave that'll pick off the survivors," he continues, getting more and more agitated. "It's the perfect sickness. It's just gonna pick us all off. Maybe it was designed like this. Maybe it's not some random virus that mutated on a pig farm in China. Maybe it's something from a laboratory".

I step toward the table. "That sounds like -"

"Stay back!" he yells, backing away from me until he's up against the wall. There's a look of absolute and total panic in his eyes.

"What's wrong?" I ask, looking back across the room.

"You might have it," he continues, clearly terrified. "For all I know, you've got it and you're gonna give it to me".

"I'm not sick," I reply. "Look at me. Do I look like there's something wrong with me?" I take another step toward him.

"No!" he shouts, grabbing a chair and holding it up to defend himself. "I swear to God, kid, if you come any closer I'll take you down. If it's me or you, I'll drop you before you can even blink".

"I'm not sick," I say again.

"You said it yourself. No-one seemed sick the other day, and then it just happened".

"Exactly!" I reply. "It happened, and we didn't get sick, so there's -"

"Get away from me!" he yells, jabbing the

chair at me before he edges his way toward the door.

"Where are you going?" I ask. "You can't just -"

"If you come anywhere near me again," he says, fixing me with a demented stare, "I'll kill you. The same goes for your brother, and for anyone else in this building, do you hear me? Spread the word. I'm not gonna let you all infect me!" With that, he mutters something else that I can't quite make out, before dropping the chair and racing off across the foyer. Shocked, I stand and listen to him as he runs through the door to the stairwell. I wish I could dismiss his rambling fear as an overreaction, but there's a part of me that worries he might be right.

# THOMAS

*Oklahoma*

IT'S HOT WITH THE gas mask on, but I don't see that I've got any other option. If I'm right about Lydia, she's liable to be infectious, which means I need to take every possible precaution. Hell, it might even be too late already. When I was in the room with her yesterday, she was a total mess; she was coughing up blood, and there was something kind of desperate about the way she lunged at me. I've seen people with flu before, and this seemed like more than flu. It was almost as if she wasn't in control of herself, like she was getting totally desperate.

"Thomas?" my mother calls out.

Turning, I see her standing at the bottom of

the stairs.

"What are you doing?" she asks.

"I'm going to check on her," I say, holding up the key in my hand. My voice sounds strange in the confines of the gas mask, and I have to speak a little louder so that I can be heard.

"Let her sleep," she replies, with a worried look on her face.

"I'm just going to make sure she's okay," I say. "I'm not going to actually go all the way inside".

"Don't you think you should wait for your father to come home?" she continues. "I don't want you going in there, Thomas. You might catch whatever she's got. I don't want you coming down with the flu as well".

"This isn't flu," I say.

"Can't you get a ladder?" she continues. "Put a ladder up outside and look through the window. That way, you don't even have to go near her. Your father must have an old ladder in the barn".

"I'll be quick," I tell her. "Stop worrying".

As I slide the key into the lock, I realize there's a strange whispering noise nearby; it takes a moment before I realize it's coming from my mother, who has started quietly saying a prayer for my safety. I turn the key and push the door open just a couple of inches, half-expecting Lydia to come rushing at me. I wouldn't blame her if she'd decided to hide and keep quiet, hoping to lure one of us into the room so she could try to escape. Stepping back for a moment, I grab an old broom that has been propped near the top of the stairs; after all, it doesn't hurt to have something I can use for defense. However, as the door slowly swings a little further open, I see a pair of bare feet sticking out from the bottom of the bed.

"Do you see anything?" my mother hisses.

"Just her feet," I reply, before taking a step toward the door. "Lydia?" I call out, but there's no reply. In fact, the feet - which otherwise look completely normal - are totally still.

"Don't go too close!" my mother calls out. "Thomas, you promised you wouldn't go all the way inside!"

"It's okay," I say, using the tip of the broom to push the door open. Lydia is on the bed, rolled onto her side and facing away from me. There's a dressing gown covering most of her body, with just her feet sticking out at one end and her head at the other. The bedsheets have been thrown aside and are gathered in a crumpled heap on the floor, with a hint of yellow and brown bodily fluids staining the fabric. Despite this, and despite the stale smell of sweat and feces, the situation looks far more normal than I'd expected, although I can see some more spatters of blood on the floor and some dark liquid in the blue bucket.

"Lydia?" I say again, starting to feel more and more certain that she's dead. The bowl of soup I brought up yesterday is still sitting untouched on the bedside table, and the air in the room seems undisturbed and stale. I take a couple of steps forward.

"What do you see?" my mother calls up from the bottom of the stairs.

"I don't know," I say. "She -" Suddenly I notice something moving; it's as if her body shifted just a fraction of a millimeter. It was such an imperceptible sight, I'm not even certain it actually happened.

"Thomas?" my mother continues.

"Hang on!" I call back to her. I'm watching the bedsheets intently, and I'm pretty sure there's an occasional hint of movement. Nothing much, but perhaps enough to show that Lydia's breathing.

"Thomas?" my mother calls up again. "Will you *please* tell me what's happening?"

"I think she's breathing," I say. Something about the shape of Lydia's body doesn't look quite right, although from this angle it might just be a result of her dressing gown being scrunched up.

"Don't get too close!" my mother reminds me. She sounds completely terrified.

"I know!" I reply, though I'm already stepping carefully around the bed, making sure to keep close to the wall while holding the broom out in front of me. There's still a chance that she might leap at me, and I need to be ready. My heart is pounding, and I'm convinced that she's just faking being asleep so she can make a run for it. As I get around to the other side of the bed, I see that her eyes are closed but that, otherwise, she actually doesn't look too bad. Whereas her skin looked kind of yellow yesterday, it's a little more normal now, although she still looks pretty sick and there's dried blood and vomit on her chin. In a way, she looks totally peaceful, although I'm keenly aware that she could throw herself at me without any warning.

"Thomas!" my mother shouts. "Thomas, don't get too close! Are you listening to me?"

"Lydia?" I say, hoping that she might open her eyes. In the space of just a couple of minutes, I've gone from being convinced that she's dead, to wondering if she might be alive, to thinking she's dead again. Carefully, I hold the broom handle out and brush the tip against her feet. She doesn't wake up, but there definitely seems to be some kind of movement, as if her chest is rising and falling in a slow and irregular manner. After a moment, I make my way to the other side of the room and see that there's a strange shape around Lydia's belly. It looks, for all the world, as if she's pregnant, though I could swear she was thin as a rake when she arrived. Then again, perhaps she was wearing tight clothes that kept everything hidden. Something about her body shape just doesn't seem quite right.

"Are you okay?" I ask, staring at her face. Leaning a little closer, I realize that one of her eyes is very slightly open; just a millimeter or so, but definitely open. "Can you hear me?" I say, still thinking that there's a chance she might be okay. Carefully, I hold out the tip of the broom and tap her shoulder, but she doesn't respond. "If you can hear me," I continue, "give me a sign. Anything. Just blink or cough or something". I tap her shoulder with the broom again, and this time I hear a strange rumbling, ripping sound coming from her belly. Whatever's going on in there, it doesn't sound right.

"The power's still off," I say, figuring there's a chance she might be able to hear me. "We still can't get a doctor, but you just need to hold on a little longer. I'm sorry we locked you in, but..." I pause as I realize the sound from her belly is continuing; in fact, if anything, it's getting a little more urgent.

"I'm gonna go now," I say, taking a step back, but -

And that's when it happens. There's a huge pop, accompanied by the sound of fabric or skin ripping apart, and Lydia's entire torso just seems to burst open, spraying blood and some kind of yellow pus all over me along with pieces of bone and various organs. I stumble back, banging into the bedside table and slipping to the ground. For a moment, all I can do is sit there and stare at Lydia's body: her face still looks so peaceful, but her chest and belly have been ripped. The force of the blast seems to have ripped several of her ribs apart, and there are pieces of her guts all over me. My brain freezes and becomes completely blank for what feels like an eternity, before I scramble to my feet and run to the door.

"Thomas!" my mother shouts, having come halfway up the stairs.

Turning to face her, I realize I must seem like something straight out of hell. I look down and see that my clothes are dripping with blood and pus, some of which is already soaking through to my skin.

# ELIZABETH

*Manhattan*

AS SOON AS I step out the front of the building, I realize that the city has changed completely. Before all of this started, the sidewalk was constantly filled with people, hustling and bustling along. It was like a river, and you had to fight your way into one of the streams. I still remember how disorientating it was when we first moved to Manhattan, and it took me a while to learn how to survive on these streets. Right now, though, the empty street is like another world.

The most striking thing is the noise. Or rather, the lack of it. I'm standing in the middle of Manhattan, surrounded by tall buildings, and you could hear a pin drop. Even the wind, which was howling through our apartment window earlier, is just making a faint whispering sound. I swear to God, if someone started talking a couple of blocks away, I think I could hear them. It's the weirdest thing to hear my own footsteps as I step further away from the door and out into the middle of the road.

Then there's the dust. Everything is covered in a thin sprinkling of white powder, and there's more coming down all the time from the overcast sky. I'm pretty sure it's from the fire that's still burning nearby where the plane crashed, which is also causing all the soot. Stopping in the middle of the street, I turn and look to the distance. All around me, little pieces of paper-like black soot are drifting down to the ground.

Walking along the street, my feet shuffling through the dust, I eventually reach the intersection. There are a few abandoned cars, and like everything else they're covered in a fine sprinkling of dust. I look in both directions and see no sign of life. It's as if everything and everyone has just stopped. I already knew, from looking out the window, that the city would be like this, but it's another thing altogether to experience it in person and to walk through the empty streets. In fact, the whole thing is so strange and eerie, I actually find myself momentarily losing all the fear and concern that I was feeling. It's unreal and surreal to be out here.

After a moment, however, I hear something. Turning and looking along the street, I see nothing but emptiness, but I know I heard voices somewhere nearby. I hurry to the next intersection, but there still doesn't seem to be anyone. Seconds later, I hear the voices again, and finally two figures appear in the distance, walking around the corner from one of the nearby streets. Instinctively, I hurry over to an abandoned car and crouch down, figuring it might not be safe to just wander over to a pair of strangers. I can hear them getting closer and closer, though, and one of them seems to be doing all the talking. It's only when they get to within a few feet that I realize I recognize the voice. Standing up, I find myself staring straight at Bob and Henry.

"Well," says Bob, stopping and grinning. "Now there's someone I didn't expect to bump into out here".

"What the hell are you doing?" I ask, turning to Henry. "I was looking for you!"

"Bob asked if I wanted to come and help him scout out the area," Henry replies, with a hint of defiance in his voice. "We've just been walking about, looking for any sign of life". He takes a rifle from over his shoulder and holds it out, as if he expects me to be impressed. "See? We're totally safe".

"Just a precaution," Bob adds, tapping his own rifle. "Never know who or what you might meet out here".

"You're wandering around with guns?" I say, shocked at the sight of my brother looking like some kind of mercenary.

"It's so we can protect ourselves," he replies. "Bob showed me how to use it, but it's only for if we get attacked". "There's little chance of that," Bob says. "As far as we can tell, the whole place is deserted, except for..." He pauses, before exchanging a concerned glance with Henry.

"Except for what?" I ask.

"We found some dead people," Henry says.

I stare at him. "Where?"

"In the..." His voice trails off, and then he turns and looks at the nearby car. "There's people in some of the cars," he says after a moment. "Not all of them, but some of them. They're dead. They're very dead".

Staring at one of the dust-covered cars, I take a deep breath as I try to come to terms with what Henry and Bob are telling me. I step forward and reach out to wipe some dust from the windshield, but Henry grabs my hand.

"I don't think you should look," he says, with a weird tone to his voice that almost makes it sound as if he thinks he's in charge. "It's pretty gross," he adds. "I don't think it's something you should see".

"I'm older than you," I say, pulling my hand

away and wiping the windshield clean. For a moment, I can't see anything other than my own reflection. Peering closer, though, I suddenly realize that there's a face staring out at me. It's a man, with his eyes wide open and his hands gripping the steering wheel. He's wearing a dark business suit, but there's something strange about the shirt. It takes a few seconds before I realize there's a huge patch of blood on his torso.

"Me and my sister have seen dead bodies before," Henry says solemnly, turning to Bob. "We saw our Grandma in the funeral home after she had a heart attack".

Turning away from the car, I take a deep breath, trying to make sure that I don't start panicking. I close my eyes, but I can still see that man's face staring at me from inside the car. The worst part is, now that I've seen a body close up, I can't help imagining what must have happened to our parents. Are they also trapped in their car, dead, somewhere between here and the airport? Suddenly the city doesn't seem empty at all; instead, it seems like a giant tomb, filled with corpses. I guess it was easy to think that the dead had magically vanished, when in reality they're just tucked away in houses and offices and cars.

"Elizabeth?" Henry asks, putting a hand on my arm "Are you okay?"

I turn and stare at him. Henry's my younger

brother. I'm in charge, and yet he's the one asking *me* if I'm okay? And he's the one holding a gun?

"I think we should probably get home," Bob says. "We need to get better organized".

"It's okay to cry," Henry says, staring at me calmly. "It's natural to cry".

"Is it" I reply, filled with a strange sense of dread at the way Henry seems to be handling this. It's as if, wandering around the desolate city with Bob, my little brother has taken on a whole new personality. He's clearly trying to seem older and more grown up, but with that rifle slung over his shoulder, he looks like some kind of parody of a man. "Thanks for letting me know" I say, looking down at his hand as it rests on my arm. Suddenly, the thought of Henry having a gun is the most sickening thing I can possibly imagine. "Give me that," I say, reaching out for the rifle.

"No!" Henry shouts, pulling away.

"Give me that gun," I say. "There's no way you're keeping it".

"Says who?" Henry replies angrily. "You're not in charge!"

"Mom and Dad put me in charge when they went away for the weekend," I remind him, reaching out for the gun again.

"They put you in charge for a couple of days," he replies, stepping away from me. "They didn't put you in charge forever. They didn't put you in charge for all of this!"

"Give me the gun," I say firmly. "Henry, I'm your sister. I'm older than you. Give me the gun".

"Hang on -" Bob starts to say.

"Give me the gun!" I shout, pushing past Bob and trying to grab Henry again.

"No!" Henry shouts, pushing me away. "You don't get to tell me what to do! You're not the boss!"

"I am!" I reply, trying to stay calm. "I'm in charge, Henry, so give me the gun! You're not old enough to have something like that. Do you know how scared I was when you just left the apartment today? I didn't know where you were!"

"I was with Bob!" he says, raising his voice. "I don't have to tell you everything I do!"

"Listen, kids," Bob says, interrupting us. "I don't think this is the time for a family argument".

"Shut up," I snap at him. "You're not helping".

"Just trying my best," he replies, taking a step back. "I tell you what I'm gonna do. I'm gonna head back to the building and see how Albert's doing with the radio, and you two kids can sort things out between yourselves and then come back and we can talk things over. Henry, do you remember what I told you about the safety catch?"

Henry nods, while keeping his eyes fixed on me.

"Is it on right now?" Bob asks.

Henry nods again, still staring at me.

"You only take it off if you're gonna use the gun," Bob continues. "Remember what I told you about gun safety. It's not a toy, Henry. It's a tool. If you don't use it properly and with respect, I'll take it back. You understand?"

"Yes, Sir," Henry says firmly.

"Okay. You've only got too cartridges in there, so remember not to fire unless you absolutely have no other choice". With that, Bob turns and starts walking slowly along the street, heading back to our building.

"I know you think you're in charge," Henry says after a moment, turning to me with a determined look in his eyes, "and I get that. You've always been in charge, 'cause you're my older sister. But you're not in charge anymore. Things have changed and you're totally not in charge right now. It was okay for a couple of days, when we were still hoping that maybe things were gonna get back to normal pretty fast, but it's not okay now. Things aren't gonna get back to normal, maybe not ever, so you're not the boss of me anymore and you can't treat me like I'm some kind of stupid little kid".

"I'm not treating you like a kid," I say.

"Yeah," he replies, "you are".

"So you think you're a man now?" I ask. "Just because you've got a gun in your hands? You think that means you're suddenly so much older?"

"Bob gave me a gun because it might be dangerous out here. Bob thinks ahead. He knows what we're dealing with and he knows what we have to do. I trust him. Would you rather I wasn't able to protect myself?"

Before he can get another word out, a gunshot rings out nearby. I turn and look first one way, then the other, but I don't see any sign of movement. Still, someone definitely just fired a weapon.

"Where was that?" I ask, feeling a kind of cold panic gripping my body.

"Come on," Henry replies, grabbing my arm and leading me along the street. As we turn the corner and hurry toward our building, Henry lets go of me and takes the rifle from his shoulder. There's a clicking sound, which I assume means that he's removed the safety catch, and he aims the rifle straight in front of us.

"Henry..." I start to say.

"Don't worry," he replies, staring intently ahead, as if he's on alert. "I've got us covered".

I want to argue with him, but instead I decide we can save the discussion for later. Right now, we have to get back to the building. However, as we get closer, I realize that there's a figure on the sidewalk up ahead. Moments later, it becomes clear that the figure is actually a dead body, with his head blown away and blood spilling out into the white dust.

# THOMAS

*Oklahoma*

"EVERY INCH!" my mother shouts, running into the bathroom and thrusting two small bottles of antiseptic wipe into my hands. "You have to clean every inch of your body," she says, hurrying over to the cupboard under the sink. She starts rifling through the various bottles and jars until finally she pulls out a can of bleach. "Maybe this," she says quietly, as if she's thinking out loud. "Thomas, you might have to use bleach".

"I'm not washing in bleach!" I say, starting to rub the antiseptic wipe onto my arms.

"Hurry!" she shouts, placing the bleach next to the bath. "You need to do your whole body!"

"Fine," I reply, "but give me some privacy,

will you? Just go and wait downstairs. I'll be there soon".

She opens her mouth to argue with me, but finally she seems to understand that I can do this without her help. She walks quickly out of the bathroom and, as I start cleaning my shoulders, I hear her running downstairs. Without water, it's not going to be easy to make sure I've eradicated every trace of Lydia's blood from my skin, but the antiseptic wipe will probably do the trick provided I don't miss any spots. Right now, it's the only option unless...

I pause for a moment.

Alcohol. Joe got some vodka and whiskey from the gas station, and alcohol works as an antiseptic. I quickly finish covering my body with the antiseptic wipe, before stepping out of the bath and quickly putting on some clean clothes. Racing out of the bathroom and past the door to the guest room, I make my way to my bedroom, where I grab yet another clean set of clothes before heading downstairs and making straight for the back door.

"Thomas!" my mother shouts. "Where are you going?"

"I know where there's something I can use!" I shout, not even stopping to explain. Instead, I race through the door and across the yard, heading for the old barrels where Joe hid his stash. It takes me a couple of minutes to get there, but I soon find a dozen bottles wedged out of sight. I get out of my clothes before loosening the lid of a bottle of vodka, pausing for a moment, and then pouring the entire bottle over my head. As soon as I'm done with the vodka, I grab a bottle of whiskey and do the same thing. There's a part of me that wants to use up all the bottles, but I figure I should probably keep some back in case we need some more antiseptic. Eventually, after I've used three bottles of whiskey and three bottle of vodka, I grab the clean clothes and get dressed.

"What the hell are you doing?" shouts a voice behind me. Before I can turn, Joe grabs me and shoves me aside. He drops to his knees and picks up one of the empty bottles, before turning to me. "What the hell did you just do?"

"I had to get clean," I say. My heart is racing, and there's no way I can deal with Joe's bullshit right now.

"You don't use *my* stuff, you little fuck-wit!" he shouts, getting unsteadily to his feet. He stares at me for a moment, before throwing an empty vodka bottle at my head. I duck out of the way just in time, and the bottle smashes against the wall of the little shed next to the barrels. "Who the fuck gave you the right to do this?" Joe screams, lurching toward me.

"Fuck off," I say, stepping out of his way and turning to go back to the house.

"Fuck off?" he screams, grabbing me and

slamming me against the shed. "Did you just tell me to fuck off?"

"I don't have time for this," I reply breathlessly. "Lydia's dead, Joe. Do you understand? She's dead. There was something wrong with her and she -"

"What the fuck are you on about?" he says, pushing me to the ground before stumbling toward the house.

"She was sick!" I shout, getting to my feet and hurrying after him. "Joe, there was something wrong with her. There was all this pus and gunk inside her, and it kind of exploded -"

"I'll explode you in a minute," he mutters, almost tripping as we get closer to the back door. "You locked her in that room. What the hell did you do that for? If she's dead, you're the one who killed her. Do you hear me? I'll stand up in front of any court in the land and testify that my brother, Thomas Edgewater, was the one who locked a poor, innocent young girl in a room and left her to die".

"No-one left anyone to die!" I shout, hurrying ahead of him and turning in an attempt to block him from reaching the door. "Joe, you're drunk. Do you really want Mom to see you like this?"

"I don't give a fuck," he says after a moment. "So Lydia was sick. So what? She was coughing. She fainted. She had to go to bed, and she got worse and worse. She was coughing all night the other night, and then -" Suddenly he pushes me back, causing me to lose my balance completely and land flat on my back in a pile of mud. Before I can get up, he's already made his way into the house and I can hear him stumbling upstairs. I struggle to catch up to him, but it's too late and I reach the top of the stairs to find him staring into the guest room.

"She's dead," I say, catching my breath for a moment.

He doesn't reply. He just stands there, open-mouthed and wide-eyes, and all the color drains from his face.

"I told you," I continue. "You need to get away from the door. We don't know how infectious it is. We might have to leave the house".

Slowly, Joe starts shaking his head. "What the fuck did you do to her?" he asks.

"No-one did anything," I say. "This just happened, about half an hour ago. You heard her coughing yesterday, Joe. You know she was sick".

"Fuck," he mutters. It's as if the sight of all the blood and pus has almost completely sobered him up. "No. Fuck. No".

"Come on," I say, grabbing a towel from the bannister and using it to cover my hand as I swing the guest room door shut. "You can't get drunk right now," I continue. "We all need to stick together. We need to work out what to do, because whatever happened to her, it doesn't make sense. It's something new. It's something dangerous".

"We need to go and talk to Mom," I tell him. "We need to work something out together, and then maybe we can decide what to do".

He shakes his head.

"What does that mean?" I ask. "Joe, we need you".

He shakes his head again. It's as if he's in total shock.

"Joe, this isn't the time to get like this," I continue. "You have to come downstairs so we can talk about what to do. You have to -"

Suddenly he pushes me to one side, turns and storms back down the stairs. I follow him through to the front room and finally into the kitchen, where our mother is sitting at the dining table. She looks terrified, as if she's been listening to everything that's been happening and she's scared of what Joe might do next. As soon as we're in the room, she stands up and edges back to the far wall.

"You're drunk," she says, her voice wavering.

"Fuck you," Joe spits back at her as he goes over to the taps and checks to see if they're working.

"There's no water," I say.

He doesn't reply; he just keeps turning the taps on and off, over and over again, as if he expects them to magically start working. After a moment, he goes to the wall and starts flicking the light switch on and off as fast as possible. There's something frantic about the way he's desperately trying to fix things, as if he thinks sheer force of will and determination will be enough.

"Nothing's working," I say, glancing over at my mother and seeing the look of fear in her eyes.

"Of course it's not," Joe replies, going back to the taps and trying them again. "Not with you two fucking idiots running things". He tries the taps a few more times, before stepping back and kicking the side of the sink. "What's wrong with this fucking place?" he shouts. "What the hell did you two do to it?" With tears in his eyes, he turns to me and I see that he's shaking with rage. "What did you do to *her*? Why did you kill her?"

"Joe -" I start to say.

"You too!" he yells, stepping toward me. "Whatever the fuck you two are doing, you're going to stop it right now!"

"We're not doing anything," I say, moving over to the other side of the kitchen.

"Don't fight," my mother says. "Please, Joe, you're drunk. You need to go and calm down -"

"No," he replies. "That's not what I need to do. I need to get those fucking grins off your fucking faces, and then I need to find that other bitch and teach her to think she can fuck with me!"

"Joe -" my mother tries to say.

"Shut up!" he shouts, pulling the table back and then slamming it against her legs. She lets out a cry of pain.

"Hey!" I shout, stepping forward.

"Keep out of this," Joe spits back at me. "You're just a kid".

Instead of saying anything, I wait a fraction of a second until he's turned back to look at our mother, and then I tap him on the shoulder. He turns to look at me again, and that's when I do it: I swing my fist at his face so hard, I swear to God I'm scared I might break my knuckles. Instead, I connect perfectly with the side of his cheek, and he tumbles back against the wall before slumping to the ground. I stand in silence for a moment, stunned that I actually managed to knock him out. I've never punched anyone before in my life.

"Sorry," I say, turning to my mother.

She pauses for a moment, and then she pushes the table away so she can step over to the door. "Let him sleep it off down there," she says eventually, with a blank expression that almost makes it seem as if she doesn't really care. "Your father can deal with him when he gets back".

"How much longer do you think he'll be?" I ask.

She doesn't reply. Instead, she simply turns and heads through to the next room, leaving me standing next to my unconscious brother while my fist starts to throb from the impact of the punch. Eventually I open the door to the pantry and drag Joe through, figuring he might as well be out of our way while he sobers up. As I step back into the kitchen, I take a deep breath and look down on my hands. It's hard not to imagine bacteria on them; millions and millions of bugs and germs, crawling all over my skin. I could spend all day and all night scrubbing myself from head to toe, but I can't shake the feeling that I'll never be entirely clean again. If this virus has shut down the world, it must be fairly easy for it to jump from one person to another. The only question, then, is how long it takes to show symptoms.

# ELIZABETH

*Manhattan*

"CALM DOWN," says Bob, stepping out of the building, still holding his rifle. "Everybody calm down!"

My mind is blank. Completely blank, as if some deep self-defense mechanism has realized that I can't possibly be expected to process the reality of the dead body. With his head seemingly blown apart, cracked open to reveal a yellowy brain and a mass of spattered blood, the corpse looks so shockingly fresh. I can even see how the thick pool of blood is still seeping into the dust, creating a kind of bright red paste. It's not until I've been staring at the mess for a few seconds that I realize the dead man's face is still half-attached, blown to one side like a discarded flap, with one eye having come loose. Finally, after what feels like an eternity but was probably only a couple of seconds, I realize that this dead body is - or was - Albert Carling.

"Who -" Henry starts to say.

"Don't look!" I blurt out suddenly, springing into action and grabbing my brother so that I can twist him around.

"Get off!" he shouts, pushing me away before stepping closer to the body. "This is the guy from the building," he says, before looking over at Albert. "Did *you* do this?"

"I'm gonna explain," Bob replies, raising his hands as if to show that he means us no harm. "When I got back just now, he was on his way out with a load of our supplies. I challenged him, and he attempted to cause me bodily harm. Therefore, I was left with no choice but to use lethal force in order to defend myself". The way he's speaking seems so formal, but at the same time almost childlike; it's almost as if he's giving a book report on how and why he blew a man's brains out. "This was self-defense," he says again, making sure to speak slowly and clearly. "Self-defense".

"Where was he going?" Henry asks.

"I don't know," Bob replies. "But you can see for yourself. He was intending to steal from us". He steps aside and holds the door open; a few bags of food are strewn across the foyer. "He was gabbling like a madman," he continues. "Kept saying we were all gonna infect him. I guess he'd decided he was gonna make it alone. I have no problem with anyone wanting to go off like that, but he was trying to take *our* food. I couldn't let that happen".

"So you killed him," I say, feeling a knot tightening in my stomach. "You didn't have to do that".

"I did what I believed to be the best thing in a difficult and tense situation," Bob continues, sounding as if he thinks he's at some kind of military tribunal, "and I based my decision on my perception of the danger at the time". He pauses for a moment to clear his throat. "I'm entirely comfortable with my actions and I'd do the same thing again. We're in a tight situation, and I'm not going to tolerate thieves".

I take a deep breath, trying to keep myself from throwing up. This whole situation is so strange, so hyper-real, that I don't really know how to react. I guess some people would turn and run, and some people would just stand and stare, and others would start ranting and shouting; my reaction is simply to stand there, wondering if I'm going to throw up or faint. I swear to God, it feels like something big is about to happen to my body, but I have no idea what to expect. Finally, and with very little warning, I take a few steps over to the wall, kneel down on the ground, and vomit. It's such a robotic reaction, like the most cliched thing to do, but I can't get the image of Albert's dead body out of my head. As soon as I've finished vomiting, I start to shake, and then eventually I have to move out of the way as the puddle of brown, partially digested food spreads toward my hands.

"Maybe you kids had better go inside," Bob says. "I'll clean up the mess".

"Come on," Henry says, reaching down to me, "let's go upstairs".

Without arguing, I get to my feet and allow Henry to lead me into the foyer. We walk past the spilled food and over to the door that leads to the stairwell; at the last moment, I glance back and see Bob leaning his gun against the wall as he prepares to deal with the mess. I know Albert seemed a little crazy, and I can totally understand why Bob had to stop him taking our food, but I still feel as if killing him was something of an overreaction. Couldn't he just have scared him off, or at worst just knocked him out? It just seems like Bob took the decision to shoot far too easily, which only heightens my fear of the guns that he and Henry are using.

"This way," Henry says, pulling my arm and taking me into the stairwell. "There's no point staring at it," he continues as we walk upstairs. "Are you feeling okay?"

I don't reply. I *can't* reply. The sight of

Albert's shattered head is going to haunt me for the rest of my life. That, and the dead body in the car, which was just as horrific. Until these two sights, I was able to make myself believe that there was still some semblance of the normal, real world left in this situation; now, it's as if we've passed a threshold and entered something entirely new, where dead bodies are rotting in abandoned cars and people get their heads blown off if they try to steal some food. I feel as if all the rules of life have suddenly been changed, and the worst thing is that I can't see a way back from this point. Now that people are actually dying, it seems as if no-one going to be able to come along and wave a magic wand to make everything alright.

"Maybe you should get some rest," Henry says as we reach the top floor and head along to our apartment. "I'll go back down and help Bob, but you should just try to sleep or something".

As we reach the door, I stop and stare at our desolate, dust-covered apartment. Something in my body starts to seize up, and I realize I can't keep going. When I see the dust on the floor, I can't help imagining Albert's blood soaking into the entire building.

"Elizabeth?" Henry says, turning to me. "Are you okay?"

"This isn't going to end any time soon," I say suddenly. "Is it?"

"What do you mean?"

"This. All of it. The lack of power. The lack of water. The empty streets. It's not some temporary passing thing. It's not a blip. No-one's gonna come riding in and save us. This is the world now, at least for a while".

"Maybe longer than that," he replies. "Maybe forever".

"Do you seriously believe that?" I ask. "Do you really, truly believe that no-one's gonna come to the rescue? Don't you think that some day soon, the power's gonna come back on and water'll start flowing from the taps again?"

"If someone was coming," he says, "wouldn't they be here by now?"

"Not necessarily. They might have limited resources. They might not know where to start, or they might be starting with Washington, or..." My voice trails off. Every time I try to put my faith into words, I end up sounding like some kind of babbling idiot; the truth, though, is that I can't lose hope.

"I'm going to help Bob," Henry says after a moment, turning and heading downstairs. "You should probably stay up here for a few hours," he calls back to me, "at least while we clean up".

"Be careful around Bob!" I shout back at him. "Henry? Be careful with those guns!"

I wait for him to reply, but there's nothing. I

guess he's decided that Bob's his best bet right now. Maybe I was a little heavy-handed earlier, and maybe I should have let him feel as if he was a little more in control. By trying to emphasize my authority, I probably just pushed him away and made myself seem like a total idiot in the process. I fucked up, but there's still time to turn things around. Nothing's forever. Good things and bad things alike, they have their time and then they end. One day this nightmare will be over, and we'll start getting our lives back into shape.

I just hope Henry doesn't do anything stupid before help comes. I feel like I've completely lost control of my brother; it's as if, by giving him that gun, Bob has gained his complete confidence and trust.

Sitting in the stairwell, I stare straight ahead and listen to the sound of Henry's footsteps getting further and further away. Despite everything that's happened, I still feel as if things are going to be okay; despite the bodies in the cars, and the burning planes, and the complete lack of intervention from the government, I'm convinced that eventually life is going to start getting back to normal. There's still a good chance that our parents are out there somewhere, making their way here. We just have to stay calm, remain in the building, and hope that sometime in the next few days there'll be a sign of things getting better. It's just not possible that the world will stay like this. Someone, somewhere, is going to intervene and make sure that things improve, and I still believe that somewhere out there, our parents are slowly but surely making their way back to us.

# DAY 4

# THOMAS

*Oklahoma*

"DID YOU PUNCH ME?" Joe says, staring up at me from the pantry floor.

"No," I say after a moment. I figure we've got enough problems without having to deal with Joe's wounded ego. "You passed out last night, so I dragged you in here".

"Shit," he continues, sitting up and rubbing the sore spot on the side of his face. "Feels like someone got me with a right-hook. I swear..." He pauses, as if he's remembering something. "I guess not. I must've taken a bit of a tumble, huh?" Grabbing hold of the side of a nearby cupboard, he hauls himself to his feet and immediately lets out a groan. "Fuck, that's not good".

"What?"

He sighs. "Nothing. I guess you know it was a good night when you can't remember a damn thing". He blinks a couple of times, as if he's trying to clear his head. "I feel like someone's ringing a bell in my head. You ever had a proper hangover?"

"Dad's not back yet," I say.

He stares at me for a moment. Even in his hungover state, he clearly understands that something's wrong. "How long's he been gone now?" he asks cautiously.

"Almost two days. He said he'd be back in one, so..." My voices trails off as I try to avoid facing the truth. The thing about our father is, he's a very straightforward kind of guy. If he says he's going to be back in one day, he'll be back in one day; the fact that he's late, even in this kind of situation, is a bad sign. The only reason I can think for him not to be back is that he *can't* get back.

"Maybe he's got a flat," Joe points out. "With his hernia, he'd have plenty of trouble fitting a fresh one. You thought to go take a drive and see if he's pulled up by the side of the road somewhere between here and town?"

"There's another problem," I say.

"Yeah?" He laughs. "Well, that sounds perfect, 'cause we just haven't got enough problems right now, have we?" Pulling the door open, he heads out into the kitchen, and then he stops again.

Slowly, he turns to me and I see there's a look of shock on his face. "Lydia," he says eventually.

"You remember what happened?" I ask.

He stares at me for a moment. "Is she -"

"Dead? Yeah. Upstairs still. I can't work out how to get her out of the house. Even if we get all the bits together and clean the room, there's no way we can clean ourselves after. But it's not like we can just leave her there, 'cause that's gonna make the whole house stink in a day or two. So we've got a real problem".

"What the fuck happened to her?" he asks. I can't work out of the color's fading from his face because he's hungover, or because he's remembering the sight of Lydia's body, or a bit of both.

"She was sick," I explain, walking over to the cupboard and grabbing one of our few remaining bottles of water. "Here," I say, "you need this". I pass him the bottle and wait while he drinks. "She got worse and worse," I continue eventually, "and eventually she could barely even stand up. She was coughing blood all day and all night, and then she stopped. That's when I went in and..." I take a deep breath as I remember the moment Lydia's body exploded all over me. "I don't know what caused it, but something about her wasn't right. She was all messed up. I'm no expert, but I'm pretty sure that's not a normal kind of sickness".

"Yeah, well..." He pauses, before walking over to the sink and staring down at the drain. After a moment, he leans down a little further before vomiting.

"I'm collecting rainwater," I tell him. "I put out some big barrels this morning. There hasn't been any rain yet, but when it comes, we should have plenty. We need food, though. We're running low".

"And where do you think I'm gonna magically get food from?" he asks.

"I thought maybe you know how to hunt".

"Hunt?" He turns to me. "Are you serious? What the hell are we gonna hunt around here? You want grilled rat brain for dinner?"

"I want *something* for dinner," I reply. "I'm starving, and we've only got enough food for about two more days. Don't you think we should start taking a look around, maybe set out some bait?"

"What the -" He stares at me. "What do you think's gonna happen, Thomas? You think we put out something tasty and we're gonna catch ourselves a cow or a nice leg of lamb? The most we could find around here - and I mean the absolute, very most - would be some kind of fucking squirrel".

"That's not true," I say. "I've listened to Dad talk over the years. We might be able to find deer and rabbit and quail. There's also some fishing equipment in the barn, so we could maybe go catch something". I wait for him to reply, but he just seems totally shocked by the idea of us going out to get food. "Come on, Joe. Do you really not know how to go hunting?"

"Of course," he says, not entirely convincingly.

"We'll take two guns," I say. "One for you and one for me".

He nods.

"But we've got another problem," I say after a moment. "Mom's -"

"We'll deal with it," he replies, "but right now, I don't know how. Let's just take one thing at a time. Doesn't Mom have a load of cleaning products? Maybe if we wrap Lydia's body in a sheet without actually touching her, we can get her out of the house and bury her somewhere. Then we can use gloves or something to pick up the bits, and then we can clean the room and maybe lock the door for a while. Then when the power and everything comes back on, we can clean properly".

"You think the power's gonna come back on?" I ask.

"Don't you?" He turns to me. "Seriously? You think this is the end of the world?"
"Sure looks that way".

He smiles. "No chance". Walking over to the back door, he steps outside and makes his way toward the barn. I watch as he goes inside and, a couple of minutes later, he emerges carrying two rifles and a box of ammunition. When he gets back over to the house, he rests the guns against the wall before opening the box and looking at the bullets.

"You know much about guns?" I ask, joining him outside.

He shakes his head.

"Didn't Dad ever teach you how to shoot?"

"Just stick a bullet in the gun, then point and shoot," he replies, holding up one of the bullets. "How hard can it be?"

He walks around to the front of the house. Following him, I eventually spot our mother, over by the washing line. She's taking down some clothes she washed before the power died, but she keeps having to stop so she can cough.

"What's wrong with her?" Joe asks, his voice sounding tense.

"That's what I've been trying to tell you," I say. "We've got another problem. It's Mom. She's sick".

He turns to me. "How sick?"

"Sick".

Over by the washing line, our mother breaks into a particularly long coughing fit.

"Like... flu sick?" Joe asks eventually.

"Like properly sick," I reply. "She says she's fine, but I'm not sure. I think she might have what Lydia had".

# ELIZABETH

*Manhattan*

"THERE ARE FIVE CONVENIENCE stores within a two-block radius," Bob says, pointing at the rough map he's sketched on the wall. "There are also two pharmacies and three restaurants. Then there are various shops, not to mention an assortment of vending machines. In other words, there's a huge amount of food potentially in the area, as well as significant quantities of bottled water and other beverages. We need to find, gather and then sort all these items and determine the correct order in which to use them. This isn't going to be an easy operation but I'm confident that, if we're smart, we can pool together a significant stockpile of food that'll last us for many months.

And that's before we start exploring further out". He stares at the map for a moment. "Then there are the bins," he adds, seemingly lost in thought. "It might be worth going through the bins".

We all sit in silence for a moment. Bob convened this little meeting so we can listen to his plan, which so far seems to be making sense. With Mrs. DeWitt having refused to leave her apartment since the disaster struck, there are basically four of us left in the building: aside from Henry and myself, there's Bob - who has somehow taken on a kind of leadership role - and there's also a middle-aged guy named Harrison Blake who keeps himself to himself and seems happy to sit at the back of the room and listen to Bob's ideas.

"So..." I pause for a moment. "You think we should go and *steal* food?" I ask eventually. "I mean, do we really need to do that?"

"Bob's right," Henry says. Frankly, at this point I think Henry would back up *anything* that Bob said. It's becoming alarmingly clear that Henry has chosen to ally himself with Bob and follow every order he's given; I guess my little brother likes holding a rifle. "We can't just sit around waiting," he continues. "We have to take action".

"What about you, Mr. Blake?" Bob says, walking past me and approaching Harrison at the back of the room. "You've been very quiet, but I'm sure a smart man such as yourself must have plenty of ideas".

Blake shrugs.

"Well," Bob says, "I propose we put things to a vote. Those who think we should follow my plan and go out to gather food, raise your hands".

Henry immediately raises his hand high into the air, and after a moment I do the same. Turning, I see that Harrison Blake hasn't move at all, and hasn't raised his hand.

"Mr. Blake," Bob says, sighing, "do you have a problem?"

"Not at all," Blake replies. "I just don't like the mob mentality. Smashing windows and pilfering food isn't quite my kind of thing".

"But eating's your kind of thing, isn't it?" Bob asks. "Drinking's your kind of thing. *Breathing's* your kind of thing. You just acknowledged that this has become a dog-eat-dog world, so I'd have thought you might be more willing to accompany us on this mission. Was I mistaken in that belief, Mr. Blake?"

"Not necessarily," Blake replies. "While I agree with you in principle, Bob, I have doubts about your long-term plan. It seems to me, and you must correct me if I'm mistaken, that you plan to gather as many supplies as possible and keep them here. It's like you're planning to turn this building into some kind of fortress".

"That would be one way of describing it,"

Bob says. "We need to give ourselves the best possible chance of surviving".

"And that's a very admirable sentiment," Blake continues, "until you realize that it's completely doomed. You'll essentially be sitting here, waiting to die. It doesn't matter how much food you scavenge and how long you think you can make it last, at some point you're gonna run out. I give you all a month, maybe three months at most, and then what? By then, the city's gonna be overrun by vermin. Think of all those dead bodies. There's gonna be disease. At the very least, rats are gonna be a big problem". He pauses for a moment. "You stay here, you die".

"And what's your alternative?" Bob asks, clearly unimpressed.

"We leave New York," Blake replies. "We head out of the city and find somewhere to start again. It's not ideal, but it's better than clinging nostalgically to New York simply because it *used* to be a good place to live. Seriously, I don't think you've got any idea how fucking awful this place is gonna get after a few weeks".

"We can't leave," I say.

"Why not?" he snaps back at me.

"Because..." I pause, realizing that I might sound stupid if I suggest there'll be other survivors. To be honest, I'm still clinging to the hope that my parents are going to somehow show up, but I can tell that Harrison Blake would shoot that idea down immediately. "Because we have resources here," I say eventually. "We can make it work".

"Bullshit," Blake replies. "Think about it. There are dead bodies everywhere. In all the buildings, in all those cars. Dead bodies don't just disappear neatly. They're gonna start to rot, and stink, and then there'll be all the rats, and before you know it, you'll be in this middle of this infectious, disgusting soup that'll just destroy everything". He smiles. "Face it. This place is going to become uninhabitable real fast, and sticking around is basically a kind of slow suicide. The sooner we pack up and get moving, the better. We're all still fairly strong, none of us seems to be sick, so we need to find the right place and start again".

There's an awkward pause for a moment as we wait for Bob to speak. He walks slowly back over to his desk and looks down at some papers for a moment, before glancing back over at us. "What are you waiting for?" he asks, acting as if he doesn't give a damn. "I'm not stopping anyone from leaving. I profoundly disagree with Mr. Blake here, but I'm not gonna stand in your way. Elizabeth and Henry, you're free to do what you want, and to go where you want. If Mr. Blake actually goes through with his plan to up sticks, that's fine by me. We need people here who are dedicated to the cause. If you want to be elsewhere, or if you think this plan of mine is a bad idea, then I'd rather you leave".

"I'm not going anywhere," I say.

"Me neither," Henry says quickly.

"You're gonna stay and wait to die?" Blake asks incredulously. "Seriously? Two young, strong, healthy people, and you're gonna just sit around and wait for the inevitable to happen?"

"It won't be like that," Henry says. "We have a plan".

"Everything's in hand," Bob says.

"And what does that mean?" Blake asks.

"It means that I have everything all planned out," Bob continues. "We can become entirely self-sufficient here, given time. Meanwhile, I want to remind you that one of our primary objectives here is to gain access to the pharmacy. They'll have useful things, like antibiotics and -"

"It won't work," Blake says, getting to his feet and walking over to the door. "I'm out. I'm gonna get my shit together and head on out of here later today. I'm gonna head south and try to find somewhere warm, and then I'm gonna set up shop on a nice piece of land and see what I can rustle up. You're all welcome to join me, but there's no way I'm staying here".

"Then there'll be more steak for the rest of us," Bob says.

"Steak?" Henry asks.

"I happen to have had some rather tender

steaks in my fridge when all of this happened," Bob explains. "Rather than try to keep it good indefinitely, I was planning to light a small fire outside tonight and cook the last of the steaks for us all. It seems only fitting. But if you won't be with us, Mr. Sharpe, I suppose that just means more for the rest of us".

"Sounds like you've got everything all worked out," Sharpe replies. He turns to walk out of the room, before stopping and glancing back at Bob. "By the way, if you're worried that I might be like Albert Carling and try to steal some of your precious food, you're way off base. I have a small stash in my apartment still, so I'll be taking supplies exclusively from there. If I have anything left over, I'll happily donate it to the cause".

Once he's gone, the rest of us sit in silence for a moment. Personally, although I could never even consider leaving the city while there's still a chance of our parents showing up, I can see Blake's point; life in New York under these conditions is going to become intolerable at some point, and eventually Henry and I are going to have to make a difficult decision. In a few weeks, or a few months, we're going to have to decide if we've reached the point at which we need to move on; that moment hasn't arrived yet, however, and I guess that means we have to work with Bob, at least for now.

"You two still with me?" Bob asks, his voice

a little quieter than usual.

"Yes, Sir," Henry replies.

After a moment, I realize they're both staring at me. "I guess," I say, my voice sounding a little weak. Looking over at Henry, I can see from the look in his eyes that he's committed to Bob's plan.

"Excellent," Bob says, grinning broadly. "Let's get going. There's no time like the present, and if we work hard all day, we can be back in time for steak by sundown".

# THOMAS

*Oklahoma*

"I'M FINE," my mother says, pulling some tins from the cupboard. "What would you boys like for your lunch? I'm afraid we don't have much, but I could heat up some beans. Desperate times call for desperate measures". She smiles, and then she lets out a small grunt, as if she's desperately trying to hold in a coughing fit.

"You sure?" Joe asks. He and I are standing in the doorway, watching for any sign of our mother's health getting worse. It's kind of a grim moment; we haven't discussed the matter, but the fact that we're standing here at all is, I guess, enough of a sign that we're both worried.

"I might have a slight cold," she says,

grabbing a can opener. "Apart from that, I think I'm doing okay, all things considered".

As she opens the first can, I look over at Joe and see the look of concern in his eyes. He might not have vocalized his fears yet, but I can tell he's thinking the same thing that I'm thinking: our mother's sick, in the same kind of way that Lydia was sick, and it's pretty clear that she's going to get worse.

"Are you boys going stand there watching me all day?" she asks after a moment. "Or are you going to go and do something useful? Thomas, are those water butts ready? I think it's going to rain soon".

"They're ready," I say.

"Perhaps you should double-check that they're clean," she continues, pouring the beans into a saucepan and taking extra care to avoid eye contact with either Joe or myself. "We don't want any contaminants getting in there, do we? I remember one year, your father got them all set up and didn't notice there were slugs in the bottom. No-one wants to drink slug water, now, do they?" She carries the saucepan over to the stove. "Excuse me," she says, hurrying through to the pantry and shutting the door. After a moment, she starts coughing; not just coughing, but really wheezing her guts up. I swear to God, the hairs on the back of my neck are standing up. It's like I've been thinking that this moment could come for a while, but it's finally here. Sometimes, I hate being right about stuff.

"She's sick," I say quietly.

"Shut up," Joe replies.

Suddenly the pantry door opens and our mother comes back out, smiling a false smile. "Now what are you two boys talking about? I could hear you whispering. Are you still worried about me?" Taking the saucepan from the stove, she hurries outside to the little brick fire our father set up before he left. Joe and I walk to the door and watch as she uses some matches and a little paraffin to get the fire going. "I wish you boys wouldn't fret," she continues after a moment. "I'm quite okay. If you're thinking that I'm going to go the same way as Lydia, I'm afraid you've got another thing coming. I'm fighting fit and ready to go. I've just got a little bit of a cold, that's all. To be honest, I was already feeling it long before Lydia turned up, I just didn't want to mention it and -" As she picks up the saucepan, her hands fumble slightly and she drops the beans all over the grass. "Now look what you made me do," she says, starting to speak faster and faster. She carefully scoops the beans back into the pan. "Well, you'll have to just work around any grass you find. We can't afford to be throwing things out, can we?"

"We're going to go hunting later," Joe says

solemnly. "We thought maybe we could find a deer or something".

"I hope your father gets back today," my mother continues after a moment. "It's not like him to miss dinner three days in a row. Still, things are probably rather hectic over in Scottsville. I bet he's been roped into all manner of jobs, keeping that place going. Your father's a smart man, you see, so he'll have seen all the things they're doing wrong. No wonder he isn't back yet. We shouldn't get too worried if he has to delay his return a little longer, should we? He might be there for -" She starts coughing again, and this time she doesn't have time to go and hide in the pantry. After a moment, she grabs a bowl, ready to serve up the beans.

"Actually, Mom," Joe says after a moment, "can you keep those beans on hold? I think Thomas and I should get going".

"But they're ready!" she says, with a look of absolute shock in her eyes.

"We'll eat them later," Joe replies, grabbing my arm and leading me away. "We can't eat those," he whispers.

"Do you think -" I start to say.

"Let's just get going," he says, interrupting me. "We're running out of daylight". We walk on in silence, but there's an unspoken understanding between us: our mother's sick, and if she's going to go the same way as Lydia, neither of us wants to be around to witness her final moments. When we get far enough away, so that she won't hear us, Joe stops by the barn and kicks the wall. "Fuck" he mutters, before turning and walking off to the back of the building, leaving me standing alone on the grass.

# ELIZABETH

*Manhattan*

"STAND BACK," Henry says, holding the butt of his rifle up against the shop door. He pauses for a moment, before slamming the butt against the window; unfortunately, the glass seems to be strengthened, and nothing happens. He tries several more times, but with no luck. "Fuck it!" he says, pausing to catch his breath.

"You won't get in like that," Bob says, sliding the safety catch from his gun.

"Are you sure you want to waste a bullet?" Henry asks. "I can keep trying".

"It's not a waste of a bullet," Bob replies, aiming at the window as Henry steps aside. "It's tactical use of one finite resource in order to gain access to a greater finite resource". There's a loud bang as he pulls the trigger, and the window in the shop door explodes, showering glass across the sidewalk. "Besides," he adds, with the sound of the gunshot still echoing in the empty street, "I've got quite a stockpile of ammo back in my apartment. Don't you worry about that".

"You thought ahead," Henry says, using the butt of his rifle to knock some of the remaining glass out of the way. He turns to me. "You hear that, Elizabeth? He thought ahead".

Standing out on the dusty sidewalk, I stare in stunned silence as the pair of them start loading their bags with produce from the shelves. It's kind of hard to believe how quickly and successfully Bob and Henry seem to have formed this bizarre double-act.

"Elizabeth!" Henry calls out to me.

Glancing over at the other side of the street, I see a couple of abandoned cars. It's hard not to think about what might be inside; are there dead bodies in every vehicle, and in every building?

"Elizabeth!" Henry shouts. "Come on!"

Reluctantly, I step through the doorway and find myself in a gloomy little convenience store. Bob and Henry have already managed to empty quite a few of the shelves into their rucksacks, so I head over to the canned goods aisle and start collecting various items. I can't quite throw my energy into the looting business with as much enthusiasm as Bob and Henry, and I still have this voice at the back of my head that keeps telling me that this is all wrong. However, in the absence of any kind of external authority - there are no cops, no government, no other people at all - I figure I need to get over my concerns and just do what's necessary. I figure I can always explain my actions to my parents if they ever come back. They'll understand.

"Put the bags in here," Bob says, having found a shopping cart at the back of the store. "We can get more in one visit. Frankly, I don't much like being out in broad daylight. We're easy pickings for anyone who happens to spot us".

"Like who?" I ask. "There's no-one else around".

"Not that we've seen so far," he replies, "but everything can change in the blink of an eye".

For the next few minutes, we load up the cart with as many things as we can. Glancing at the dates on the cans, I see that some of them are good for another two years, and I try to imagine us still sitting around here after all that time, still waiting to be rescued. Still, it's starting to look as if we're not going to starve, even if our options are going to be fairly limited.

"This is so cool," Henry says as he walks past me.

"Cool?" I ask, turning to him.

He drops a load of cans into the shopping cart. "Well, kind of," he replies. "I mean, it's kind of cool to be able to just come in and take what we want. I don't mean that everything's cool". Spotting something behind me, he hurries over and pulls a bunch of gift cards away from a display. "There's, like, two thousand dollars' worth of cards here," he says, his eyes wide with glee. "Can you imagine getting two grand?"

"And how are you gonna use them?" I point out. "There's no electricity".

"Maybe one day".

"They're useless, Henry. They're not even worth the plastic they're printed on".

"I guess," he replies, before stuffing them into his pocket. "Then again, you never know". He hurries back over to join Bob, and I watch for a moment as they continue to grab everything they can find and stuff it into the cart. After a few minutes, the cart is filled to the top and Bob grabs another from the back, and the whole process is repeated a couple of times until finally we've got three full carts, which we proceed to wheel back to our building. I've got to admit, it feels kind of good to see our stash of food go from being scarily low to suddenly being filled with all kinds of items, and it's not even midday yet. If we keep this up until sunset, we can be sitting pretty by the end of the day.

"We'll go to the pharmacy next," Bob explains, leading us back out onto the sidewalk. "There are a few nearby, but there's a bigger one about five blocks away. I figure we might as well go for the mother-load. We need pain-killers, antiseptics, bandages, things like that. In the current situation, even a relatively minor wound could become a big problem if it's not treated properly". He glances over at us as we keep walking. "You know what? I'm starting to think we make a pretty good team".

Henry smiles, and I can see that this means a lot to him. It's strange to note how quickly Henry has adapted to this new life, and how much he seems to enjoy his new role as Bob's deputy. With a rifle slung over his shoulder, he looks almost like one of those child soldiers from the news, and I can't help wondering how far he's willing to go in order to keep Bob happy. In barely four days, my little brother has gone from being a couch potato to being a gun-toting, order-taking little authoritarian. I had no idea people could change so quickly.

"Stop!" Bob says suddenly, holding out a hand to stop us in our tracks. There's an urgent, concerned tone to his voice, as if he's seen something that worries him. My initial reaction is that he's just being over-cautious, but I've got to admit that there's something pretty spooky about these empty streets.

Henry immediately takes the rifle from his shoulder, removes the safety catch, and holds it out in front of us. "What?" he asks. "I don't see anything".

"There's the pharmacy," Bob replies, "but do you see what I see?"

Looking along the street, it takes a moment before I realize that the window of the pharmacy appears to have been smashed. The rest of the shops haven't suffered any damage, so it looks as if someone has deliberately broken into the place, which means there are definitely other people alive in the city. After nearly four days of feeling as if we're alone, it's kind of shocking to find the first evidence that we're not the only survivors. At the same time, I'm filled with conflicting thoughts: on the one hand, I want to find these other people and find out what they know, but I'm also worried that they might be dangerous. Suddenly, and surprisingly, I'm forced to accept that Bob might have been right when he said we needed weapons; he said he didn't have a spare gun for me, but he offered me a hunting knife, and now I'm thinking maybe I should have accepted.

"Let's take this nice and slow," Bob says, raising his rifle. "Remember, there's no need to escalate the situation. It's quiet probably nothing, but this isn't the time to take risks. Let's just be a little cautious and keep from making any rash decisions". He looks over at Henry. "Can I trust you, boy? You're not gonna go doing anything stupid, are you?"

"No, Sir," Henry says, a look of fierce determination on his face.

"You follow my lead. Understood?"

"Yes, Sir".

"Let's just go," I say, keeping my voice down. "We can go to one of the other pharmacies. Why do we have to go barging into this one?"

"If there are other agents on the ground in this area," Bob says coldly, "I want to know".

"Other *agents*?" I stare at him for a moment. I can't help feeling that this guy is getting a little full of himself. "What are you talking about?"

"The girl waits here," Bob says after a moment.

"The girl?" I reply, raising my eyebrows.

"This is potentially a combat situation," he says. "You're unarmed, and in the event of an engagement with the enemy, we don't need to be worrying about your position. You could get caught in the crossfire, or you could be used as a hostage. It's best to keep the field of combat clean. Stay here and wait for the all-clear from us, okay? If anything goes seriously wrong, make your way back to the building, but be careful that you're not followed. We don't want anyone finding out primary location". He pauses for a moment. "I'm sorry,

Elizabeth. I shouldn't have referred to you as the girl. That was insensitive of me. I hope no offense was taken".

"It's fine," I say quietly, stepping back into a nearby doorway so that 'the boys' can get on with what they're doing. Bob and Henry move slowly and carefully toward the pharmacy, with Bob taking the lead and Henry taking up the rear. I've got this horrible, knotted, twisted feeling in my gut as I watch my little brother carrying a gun into what could be a dangerous situation, but I know better than to try arguing; at least Bob seems to be fairly sensible, so hopefully he's going to keep things under control. Besides, if the glass had been broken recently, we'd probably have heard it; whoever was here, they're probably long gone by now.

"Hello?" Bob shouts, once he and Henry are just a few meters from the pharmacy. "We mean you no harm. Is anybody in there?" He waits for a moment, but there's no reply. "We're armed!" he calls out. "However, this is purely for our protection, and you have no reason to be worried. If you're in there, I would ask that you emerge with your hands clearly held out in front of you. Again, we mean you no harm, but we need to be certain that you have no ill intentions toward us".

Nothing.

Silence.

"We're coming inside!" Bob shouts. "Again,

we mean you no harm and all I ask if that you identify yourselves at the earliest possible opportunity. If you choose not to do so, we cannot and will not be held accountable for any mistakes that occur".

As I watch Bob step through the broken window, followed by Henry, I can't help but feel worried. Even though it seems as if the other people are long gone, I'm starting to realize that the city is potentially a huge death-trap. There might be other people out there; even worse, those 'other people' might be like Bob, in which case we need to be careful. The last thing we need is to come across a bunch of scared, panicky guys with guns. There's definitely potential for a bad situation to develop, and for a simple misunderstanding to lead to something far more serious. I've never liked guns, and the idea of my little brother wandering through a ruined city with a rifle is something I'd rather not contemplate.

After a few minutes, with Bob and Henry having been inside the pharmacy for a while, I start to wonder whether I should go and join them. Bob told me to wait until I was given the all-clear, but I guess it's possible that they've simply forgotten about me. Just as I'm about to start tentatively making my way across the street, however, I spot movement up ahead, and suddenly a girl climbs out of the pharmacy. She's looking back inside, as if she's making sure that Bob and Henry haven't seen her, and then she darts quickly along the sidewalk. She looks young, about my age, but she's stick-thin and she's wearing what appears to be some kind of old-fashioned night-dress; she also has the most strikingly white hair I think I've ever seen, and the lack of visible roots suggests it's real rather than dyed. She looks so strange, though, that it takes me a moment to be sure that I'm not imagining the whole thing.

"Hey!" I call out as she gets closer.

Looking up, she stares at me with an expression of wide-eyed horror, before turning and bolting along the street.

"Hey!" I shout, running after her. I'm not exactly in great shape, but to my surprise I find that I can catch up to her fairly easily. A couple of seconds later, I reach out and grab the back of her dress just as we head around the next corner. She's so light on her feet, I'm able to pull her back toward me. At the last moment, she slips and lands hard on her back, letting out a gasp of pain. A collection of pill packets from the pharmacy spills out across the ground. For a moment, we stare at one another in silence.

"Are you okay?" I say eventually, standing breathlessly over her.

"Elizabeth!" shouts Henry from the next street. "Elizabeth! Where are you?"

The girl starts to get up, with a panicked look in her eyes.

"It's okay," I say. "We're here like you. We're just looking for things. We're not going to hurt you".

Ignoring me, the girl starts gathering up the packets she dropped. Reaching down, I start helping her, and finally I hand her the rest of her stuff. She pauses for a moment before accepting them, and then she turns and starts running again. Although I want to go after her, I figure she's totally spooked by the sound of Henry calling after me; moments later, I hear footsteps nearby and I turn to find Henry running along the street, with the rifle in his hands, while Bob hurries a little way behind him.

"Who was that?" Henry shouts, staring into the distance as the girl disappears around the next corner.

"I don't know," I say, "but she came out of the pharmacy".

"Impossible," he replies. "We swept that place. There was no-one in there".

"Well *she* was in there," I tell him. "I watched her come out through the window a few minutes after you two went in".

"Did she hurt you?" he asks, raising his rifle as if he's expecting someone to come back around the far corner.

I shake my head.

"We're not alone," Bob says as he reaches us. He's so out of breath, he has to lean against the wall for a moment. For someone who apparently wanted to make sure he was ready for the end of the world, he sure doesn't seem to have put a lot of effort into personal fitness. "Wherever that scrawny little thing came from, you can bet she wasn't alone. There'll be more of them, and now they know we're here. They'll start poking their noses around, you can count on that".

"She wasn't dangerous," I point out. "She was just scared".

"Scared people are *always* dangerous," Bob says. "They're the ones who panic and do dumb things without thinking. They're the ones who'll sneak up behind you when you're not looking and cut your throat. It's good that she's gone; the last thing we need is another mouth to feed. On the other hand, I don't like the idea that she might be going back to tell other people about our location. Did you see what she was carrying?"

"Just some boxes of pills," I reply.

"I figured," he says, sighing. "We need to protect our supplies much more carefully. There are going to be scavengers around, and some of them are gonna form into little gangs. From now on, someone's going to have to stay behind in the building at all times. We can't risk having someone going storming in there and stealing our supplies.

We need round-the-clock surveillance and we need to make sure we're properly armed for any eventuality".

"I don't think she was going to steal anything from us," I say.

"You don't know that for sure," Bob replies, clearly puffed up on his own sense of self-importance. "Elizabeth. Henry. I believe we've just sighted our first potential enemy in this situation".

# THOMAS

*Oklahoma*

A GUNSHOT RINGS OUT, and the rabbit immediately bolts off into the distance as a cloud of soil is kicked up a few meters away.

"I never said I was a crack shot," Joe says, lowering the rifle.

"Can I try next time?" I ask.

"I'm getting better," he says firmly. "Each time, I get closer. Wait and see".

We walk on in silence for a moment. I'm not sure I really follow Joe's logic, but I don't have the energy to argue. I guess the law of averages means he's going to hit something eventually.

"So Mom seems worried," I say after a while. "Do you -"

"Let's just keep focused on what we're doing," he says firmly. "We're not out here to talk about Mom. We're out here to try to catch something to eat. Keep your mind on the job at hand".

"Yeah, but -"

"I'm serious!" he replies, raising his voice a little. "Let's just deal with problems as and when they arise, okay? She's just got a cold, that's all. It's probably stress. Nothing more sinister than that. She'll cough for a few days and then she'll be fine". We walk on a little further. "Besides," he continues after a while, "why should she get sick when we're both fine? Out of the three of us, she had the least contact with Lydia. I mean, you're the one who got exploded all over, aren't you?"

"Maybe only certain people get it," I point out, "or maybe -"

"I'm not kidding, Thomas," he says firmly. "I really don't think there's any point talking about this right now. She's gonna be fine, and if she's not, then she's not. Do you really think, out of all of us, she's the one who'd get sick? The woman washes her hands every ten seconds, and she barely went close to Lydia. If anyone was gonna get sick, it'd be me or you, so let's just focus, okay? I swear to God, you're a whiner sometimes". With that, he takes a right turn and marches away from me, as if to make doubly sure that I can't argue with him.

"Fine," I mutter, making my way through the undergrowth. I should have known better than to think I might actually have a proper discussion with my brother; he's always preferred to run away from things when they get too much, with his grand strategy being to only come back once someone else has sorted out the problem. I hope he's right about our mother being okay, but I can't help thinking it's too much of a coincidence that she's getting ill right after Lydia turns up. If that's the -

Suddenly I stop dead in my tracks. Staring straight ahead, I see a shape in the grass, and I immediately realize that it's a person, wearing what looks like a sheriff's uniform. Although I can't make out any details, I have no doubt at all that it's a dead body; as well as the flies buzzing in the area, there's also a pretty horrific smell.

"Joe!" I shout, keeping my eyes firmly fixed on the corpse. "Get over here!"

"Keep your voice down!" he replies, hurrying toward me. "You're gonna scare off any -" He stops speaking as he reaches me and sees what I've found. "Fuck," he says quietly. I guess even my loud-mouthed brother can occasionally have the wind taken from his sails.

"He's dead, right?" I say.

"I hope so, for his sake," Joe replies as he moves around the body a little to get a better view. "Jesus Christ, he stinks".

Edging a little closer, and covering my nose to reduce the smell, I see that the flesh of his left hand is a kind of dark gray color. I really don't want to see the rest of him.

"Fuck, do you know who this is?" Joe says after a moment.

"Who?"

"It's Robert Haims," he replies. "You remember the cop we found the other day? Remember how you said he'd gone from his car when we drove back past, and I said you were talking out of your ass? You were fucking right, man. This is him. He must have crawled all the way out here. Fucking incredible". Breaking a branch from a nearby tree, Joe gets ready to prod the body.

"Wait!" I say. "What are you doing?"

"Relax," he says, swatting some flies away from near his face. "The guy's clearly long gone".

"If he's got the same thing Lydia had, he might burst," I say. "She only exploded when I poked her".

Dropping the branch, Joe takes a step back. "Well that's the last thing we want, isn't it? Some damn cop blowing his guts all over us".

Staring at the body, I watch as flies crawl all over the fabric of his police uniform.

"How do you think he got here?" I ask eventually. "There's no way he could have crawled here, right?"

"Reckon there is," he replies. "If he kept going all day and all night, until finally he just dropped dead where he fell, I suppose he could've made it this far. Doesn't seem like there's any great mystery about it".

We stand in silence for a moment. It's hard to believe that this guy could have crawled so far into the forest, especially when he seemed so sick when we saw him by the side of the road three days ago. Then again, if he was trying to get help, I suppose he might have found the strength from somewhere. But there's nothing out here, not for miles around.

"That must've been a horrible way to die," I say eventually.

"Yeah, well..." Joe pauses for a moment, before turning to walk away. "He was a cop. Come on. There's nothing for us to do here".

Following Joe, I can't help glancing back at the body. Something about this whole situation just feels a little wrong. If Robert Haims wanted to get help, why would he have crawled away from the road and deep into the forest? He was a local guy, so he must have known that there was nothing here. I guess he must have just been delirious; otherwise, there's no reason why he'd have crawled so far through the undergrowth, when the only thing for miles around here is our farm, and there's no reason for him to make his way out toward us. Something about this whole thing doesn't quite make sense yet.

# ELIZABETH

*Manhattan*

AS SOON AS the phone is switched on, the signal indicator starts to load and I wait with baited breath. Every day, just after lunch, I come to my bedroom and test to see if either the phone or internet system has managed to get up and running again. I keep thinking that one day, suddenly, out of nowhere, I'll get some bars of signal and I'll be able to communicate with someone. Anyone. But it never happens. For the fourth day running, there's no signal out there. The phone gives up, returning a 'Signal Failed' message before the battery indicator flashes critical and the system shuts down. I guess that's the end of that, then. The phone's out of power and I have no way to charge it up again. It's just a useless piece of plastic.

"Hello?" calls out a voice in the hallway.

My initial instinct is to panic, before I realize after a split second that I recognize the voice. Getting off the bed, I walk over to the door and head into the front room, where Harrison Blake is standing with a small rucksack over his back. He's wearing a thick coat and a hat, and it looks as if he's ready to get going on his journey. He said earlier today that he was planning to leave, but I wasn't sure he'd actually go through with such an insane plan.

"Hi," I say. I've only seen Blake a couple of times, and never one-on-one, so this feels a little awkward.

"I just came to say goodbye," he replies, setting the rucksack down on the chair by the door, "and to give you this. It's some food and stuff that I won't be able to carry, so I figured I should give it to someone who can use it".

"You're giving away food?" I ask.

"I figure it's better for me to be able to move fast, rather than to load myself down with too much stuff". He opens the top of the rucksack, revealing some packets of candy. "It's really not much. Nothing nutritious. But I guess sugar's always useful, right? Suddenly junk food isn't junk anymore". He smiles awkwardly, before closing the bag back up. "Anyway, I wanted to give it straight to you, rather than letting Bob fucking Sullivan get his greedy hands on it. The man's already stashing more food than he'll ever need, and I figured you might need some insurance. You don't want to put your survival in someone else's hands".

"Thanks," I say, finding the whole situation to be a little weird, "but I don't have anything to give you in return".

"That's okay. I wasn't looking for anything. I just thought it might be good for you to not be completely dependent on Bob. There's something about that guy that I really don't trust, and I don't really like the idea of him having control over everything in this building".

"He's definitely a little odd," I reply.

"He's not odd," Blake says. "He's dangerous. I've seen guys like him before. Small-minded people with a deep inferiority complex and a sense of resentment. They watch the world with hatred and they develop complex paranoid fantasies. Usually, they just waste away in their pathetic little lives, but sometimes something changes and they see an opportunity to shine. And then... And then this all happens, and suddenly - completely by accident - people like Bob are actually in a decent position. The guy's been storing ammunition away for years. He's got boxes and boxes of the stuff in his apartment. Doesn't that strike you as odd?"

"It's useful," I point out.

"It's a sign of paranoia," he replies.

"It's kind of useful".

"The guy's borderline mentally ill".

"Maybe," I say, "or maybe he just saw all of this coming a little better than the rest of us". I pause, realizing how crazy it feels to actually be defending Bob. "He's not perfect," I continue eventually, "but then, who is?"

"Listen," he says, "I know this is gonna come totally out of left-field, but I figured I should at least ask. Are you sure you don't want to come with me?"

"With *you?*"

"Yeah. I mean, I don't really know where I'm going, but I figure the city's a dangerous place to be right now. You're welcome to join me, and your brother too. I guess there's not much chance of him coming, but..." His voice trails off. "Sorry. You're right. This is a crazy idea, isn't it?"

"I have to wait here for my parents," I reply. "There's still a chance that they might make it here from the airport. I have to at least give them a few more days before..." I take a deep breath. The day's coming when I might have to reconsider my belief that they're still alive, but I don't have to face that moment yet. "Thanks for your offer," I say, "but I can't go. Not right now".

"Okay," he says. "Well, I'm just gonna head off. I hope things work out for you, Elizabeth. Stay safe".

"You too," I reply.

He pauses once again, almost as if there's something else he wants to say, and then he smiles and heads out of the apartment. I stand and listen to his footsteps as they get further and further away, and then I go to the rucksack and carry it through to my bedroom. Tipping it out onto my bed, I find that it's basically full of candy and potato chips, although at the very bottom there's a tatty old paperback book. The cover of the book has been ripped away, and the spine has been torn, while it seems that some of the early pages are also missing. After checking for a moment, I realize that there's no way to work out the title of the book, or who wrote it. In fact, with all the front material missing, the very first page is the start of the first chapter:

*The creature reached out and felt the confines of its new world. Trapped in a thin, velvety cocoon, the creature struggled and struggled until finally it made a hole in the side of its prison, and it was able to wriggle to freedom. The first thing it saw was a vast and beautiful lake, under a bright, shining sun. Making its way to the edge of the water, the creature looked down and saw, for the first time, its own reflection. Its face had changed so much.*

Flicking through the book, I struggle to work out what it's about. My first instinct, when faced with a new book, is always to go online and look it up, and to read all about the person who wrote it and about the different themes and ideas that other people have noticed. This time, though, I've got no such option; sitting on the bed, it's just me and a faded old paperback that has had its title and other details removed. Finally, I turn the book over and see that Blake has taped a key to the back page, next to which he's written a short message:

*I've left something for you in my apartment. Something I can't take with me, but which might save your life one day. Keep it to yourself.*

Taking a deep breath, I get off the bed and head out into the corridor. With Henry and Bob probably busy downstairs, I guess I have plenty of time to go and find out what Blake's message means. I head down in the stairwell until I reach one of the lower levels, and then I walk along to Blake's front door. The key fits the lock, of course, and I step into his apartment. Since his window isn't broken, Blake's apartment is a little warmer than my parents', and it immediately feels less chaotic. I carefully push the door shut before walking through to his front room.

And that's when I see it.

Or rather, *them*.

Hundreds and hundreds of them.

All four walls are covered, wherever possible, with bookshelves, and the shelves are absolutely packed with books. Looking at the ones near where I'm standing, I see that he has not only an extensive library of fiction, but also some non-fiction. He has books about history, and about medicine, and about science; he has reference books and maps and guides to nature; he even has recipe books, and books that explain how to build things. It takes me a moment to realize that Blake was right: the books in this place really could save my life one day. With no internet and no TV, the only way to get hold of information is to find old books. And that's what he's given me: a huge repository containing hundreds, possibly even thousands, of books on a wide variety of subjects, not only on bookshelves but also stacked up in the corridors. Hidden from the others. All mine.

# THOMAS

*Oklahoma*

WE CAN HEAR the coughing before we get home. As soon as we reach the edge of the forest, just a couple of hundred meters from the back of the farmhouse, the sound of my mother hocking her guts up is unmistakeable. It sounds chesty, as if she's got something in her lungs that she just can't bring to the surface. It's the exact same sound I heard the other day when Lydia was sick.

Glancing over at Joe, I see the look on his face: pure fear, born of the realization that the situation is serious. We make eye contact briefly, and I can tell that he's not ready to face this. I don't know whether it's easier or harder for him; he only saw the aftermath of Lydia's death, whereas I saw pretty much all of it. I guess neither of us is prepared for this moment. Light rain has been falling for the past few minutes, and the dry grass smells strong and sweet; at a time like this, our mother would usually be at the back door, calling for us to get home before we're soaked. But not today.

"I'm going to check the barn," Joe says after a moment, his voice dulled and sullen. He turns and starts stomping across the wet grass.

"Why?" I call after him.

"There might be more guns. We need to keep them safe".

I stand and watch as he disappears through the barn's open entrance. I want to go with him; I want to lose myself for hours and hours in a bunch of trivial jobs, but I know I have to go into the house. Our mother might be dying, and she shouldn't have to do that alone. Reluctantly, I walk over to the back door, before pausing to listen to the sound of her coughing. I guess I'm probably imagining things, but it almost sounds worse than it was a couple of minutes ago.

"Hey," I say as I walk through the door.

Startled, she looks over at me. I guess she didn't hear me coming, not over the sound of her own coughs. She's sitting at the kitchen table, with her notebook in front of her. I can immediately see that she's sick: her skin seems pallid and withdrawn, and her eyes are filled with apprehension. It's as if the sickness has tightened her skin a little, drawing her in so that her bones are more prominent. She smiles, but it's the worst smile ever: false and hopeless. The pages of her notebook are discolored by a faint spray of blood; she quickly turns to a fresh page, but it's too late. I saw.

She knows.

I know.

Whatever this thing is, it's inside her.

"How was the -" she starts to say, before coughing again. It's shocking to hear how much worse she's become in just a few hours. It sounds like she's trying to bring up some huge ball of phlegm that'll never come out.

"We didn't catch anything," I say, walking over to the table. I want to hug her but, at the same time, I'm scared to touch her.

"Don't come too close," she gasps, keeping her hands over her mouth. "I don't want you to -" She starts coughing again, and I see a little more blood dripping down onto her notebook. This is how it was with Lydia; this is *exactly* how it was with Lydia. She turns the page again, as if she thinks that a fresh, clear page is somehow a sign that she's not sick.

"Does it hurt?" I ask.

"No," she says quickly. "Not at all". She picks up her pen, takes a deep breath and starts writing in the notebook.

"What are you -" I start to ask.

"A story I've had in my head for a while," she says quickly, having anticipated the question. "Actually, I've been thinking about it for years, since before you and your brother were born. I thought I'd better finally get it down". She coughs again. More blood comes out and splatters over the page, and she quickly turns to a fresh sheet of paper and continues to write.

Grabbing a bottle of water from the cupboard, I place it next to her on the table. She pushes it aside.

"You need to drink," I tell her.

She shakes her head. "No point wasting water on me".

"No-one's wasting water," I reply, pushing the bottle back toward her. "It's raining. We'll have more soon".

"Is it?" she asks, turning to look over at the open door. "Oh. I hadn't noticed". She pauses, with tears in her eyes. "You're right. I can smell it. Petrichor".

"Petrichor?"

"The smell of rain after a dry spell. It's called petrichor. I learned that at school. Petrichor".

"I didn't know that," I say.

"Well, now you always will, won't you?" She sniffs back the tears. "Even when you're an old man, you'll still know the word petrichor. Try to remember it. It's one of those words that you can use to impress people". She starts coughing. Again, blood drips down onto the page; again, she turns to a fresh sheet of paper before she starts writing again. I can't help but notice that her handwriting seems sharper suddenly, with narrower angles and fewer loops; I guess she can't hide the tension in her body.

"I've been thinking," she says after a moment, "and I don't think you should stay here. You and your brother should get on out of this place and head to Scottsville".

I shake my head. I know what she's trying to do, but I'm not going to let her push us away.

"Be sensible, Thomas. I raised you to be sensible".

She starts coughing again. This time, when she turns to a fresh page in her notebook, she reaches the end. There are no more pages. "Don't be stupid, son," she says after a moment, staring down at her pen. "Look at me. I've got what that girl had. Whatever it is, there's nothing we can do about it, and I don't want you seeing that kind of thing again. It was quite horrible". She pauses for a moment, and I can tell that she's not going to back down. If there's one thing I know about my mother, it's that she stubbornly puts her family first in every situation, no matter how badly it might affect her. In fact, in all my life, I don't think I've ever known her to back down in an argument. "I've been thinking about it," she continues, her voice wavering slightly, "and I've made my mind up. I want you to go to Scottsville and find your father, and don't any of you come back here until you're absolutely certain that everything's okay. You'll need disinfectant and bleach in order to -"

"We're not leaving," I say firmly, starting to feel angry. Why does she keep talking like this? There's no way Joe and I can just abandon our mother to die slowly and painfully like this. "We'll take you to Scottsville," I say after a moment. "We'll put you in the other truck and we'll drive you there. There's got to be a doctor who can -"

She shakes her head.

"No, we can do it!" I continue. "We'll take you to town, and we'll find someone who knows what to do to help you! The problem with Lydia was that we didn't know what to do. You can't just give up like this! We'll take you with us. It makes sense. It's the best way to help you".

"You're grasping at straws," she replies, before coughing again. "I don't know what's happening, Thomas, but you have to face facts. It's something very, very bad, and it's beyond our control. You saw what happened to Lydia, and I don't... I don't want you to see the same thing happen to me. I've asked God to spare me, but I don't think he's listening. I don't think he's listening to any of us". She takes a deep breath, as tears start to roll down her face. "Or maybe he's listening, and this is his answer, but the only thing that will make this bearable is if I know that you and Joseph are safely on your way. I've sat here for hours and thought about it. Please, Thomas, just for once do what I ask".

"She's right," says a voice over by the door.

Turning, I see Joe staring at us. I don't know how long he's been standing there, but he has a solemn look on his face. For the first time in my life, I can see a real family resemblance between him and our mother.

"Listen to your brother," my mother says, smiling at me through her tears. "He's right, Thomas. This is no time for sentimentality or for stupid gestures. You saw what happened to that poor girl, and it's going to happen to me".

"When Dad comes back -" I start to say.

"He's not coming back," she replies, before pausing for a moment. "If he was coming back, he'd be here by now. I don't know what happened to him. I don't suppose I'll ever know, but he's obviously caught up in all of this. When you go to Scottsville, you have to be careful. Don't take any unnecessary risks".

"We're not leaving yet," I say. "It's too late in the day. We'll wait until morning". Turning to Joe, I can see that he knows I've got a point. "Think about it. We're better off waiting until dawn and leaving then. That way, we can be in Scottsville in the afternoon. It makes no sense to go off when it's already getting dark".

"I don't want you here," our mother says quietly. "I don't want you getting whatever I've got".

"We'll be careful," I say, "and anyway, if we were going to get it, we'd have it by now. Joe was kissing Lydia before we realized she was sick, and I was standing right next to her when she exploded. For some reason, we're both immune, or at least it's harder for us to get infected. So we can wait until morning".

"I'll sleep in the barn," Joe says. "The house is too dangerous".

"You sleep in the barn too," my mother adds, staring at me. "You know it makes sense, Thomas. In the morning, you can set off and go to Scottsville. I'll be okay here. You know I can always manage. What will happen, will happen, regardless of anything we try to do to stop it".

Sighing, I realize she's saying whatever she thinks she needs to say to get us to leave. She's scared of infecting us, and she's willing to just stay here alone at the farm and wait to die, rather than do anything that might cause us to become sick.

"I'm going to check on you in the morning,"

I say eventually, fighting back the tears. "Before we leave, I'm going to make sure you're okay".

She smiles sadly. "That'd be nice".

There's an awkward silence for a moment, as if none of us can say what we're thinking. It's pretty clear that, barring miracles, she's going to be dead within a day, yet no-one can quite bring themselves to say goodbye.

"I'm going to bed," I say, walking over to the door. "I'll be in the barn".

"You should eat something," my mother calls after me.

"I'm not hungry," I say, turning back to face her. I know in my heart that this is the last time I'll ever see her, but I'm not ready to face that reality quite yet. "I'll see you tomorrow," I say eventually, as if saying the words will somehow make them come true.

"See you tomorrow," she replies.

I take a deep breath. "I'll see you tomorrow," I say again, before turning and hurrying out of the house and across the yard. By the time I reach the barn, I've managed to force the tears back; I'm not going to cry, not yet. As I clear a space on the cold concrete and sit down, I stare out at the house and think of my mother and Joe still standing in the kitchen, discussing things. For a moment, I'm able to trick myself into thinking that everything's going to be okay, that everything's normal. It doesn't last long, though. There's so much I don't know about what's happening, but there are a few certainties starting to make themselves clear: our father is gone, and our mother isn't going to be around for much longer.

"See you tomorrow," I say quietly, fixing my eyes on the house.

# ELIZABETH

*Manhattan*

WITH THE LIGHT beginning to fade, I look up from the book and realize that I'm going to have to go to sleep soon. Gone are the days when reading into the night meant flicking the switch on a lamp; these days, even light is a precious commodity.

I'm sitting in Harrison Blake's apartment, reading a book about the history of New York. While this might seem like a strange place to start, my reasoning for choosing this particular book is actually quite simple: I want to see if there are any old or forgotten parts of the city that might be useful, particularly underground. Over the years, I've heard various stories about the sewers and about how there are large caverns buried beneath the city; although I don't know exactly how these might help, I figure it'd be useful to know what's down there. Closing the book, I look over at the shelves and realize that I've got a huge job on my hands: I need to work out which books are going to be most useful, and then I need to find as much time as possible to read them. I'll never get through everything, of course, but I feel as if I need to cram my mind with as much knowledge as possible. I was never much of an avid reader before; things have changed, though, and my priorities have shifted. Frankly, I think I need a bigger head.

In theory, there's no reason why I shouldn't tell Henry about Blake's library, but I know he'd just go and tell Bob. I get the feeling that Bob's the kind of person who'd just see the books as something to be burned for warmth. It's probably too much of a stretch to think that I can keep the library hidden from him forever, but I figure I can do my best for now.

Slipping quietly out of the room, I head along the corridor and into the stairwell. I go down to the foyer, which is already pretty gloomy, but there's no sign of either Henry or Bob. Walking to the door, I look out into the empty street and I can't help thinking about Harrison Blake, walking away from the city on his journey to find a new place. There's a part of me that thinks it might have been a mistake to stay behind, but there's no way I can leave until I'm certain that my parents aren't coming back. Besides, there's no way Henry would come with me, so I guess I have no choice but to stay. Now that he might very well be my only family, I can't contemplate ever leaving him, even if staying seems like a mistake.

"Where the hell have you been?" Henry shouts suddenly, emerging from the stairwell.

"Busy," I reply, turning and seeing the worried look on his face.

"We thought something had happened to you," he replies, storming over to me. "We thought you'd gone outside and got lost, or worse!"

"I was fine," I reply. "I don't have to tell you everything I do". I smile, thinking back to the argument we had yesterday when Henry went off with Bob. Henry kept telling me that I had no right to demand to know his whereabouts all the time, and now the tables are turned.

"You have to tell us when you're going out," he continues. "We need to know where you are. We're a unit now. We have to stick together".

I stare at him for a moment. "Do you realize how much you're starting to sound like him?" I ask eventually.

"Like who?"

"Like Bob".

"You don't know what you're talking about," he replies.

"What have you been doing?" I ask, trying to change the subject.

"Come on," he replies, with a slight grin crossing his face, "I'll show you". He leads me through to the office and then to a store-room at the back of the building, where Bob has set up a small gas-powered stove. A small, slightly dry-looking steak is sizzling on the grill, but the smell is amazing: having sat upstairs for so long, I kind of didn't notice how hungry I was getting, but now I have to force myself to keep from snatching the meat away. After a few days of eating dry, pre-packaged goods, the sight of a steak is kind of overwhelming.

"It's yours," Bob says, standing in a nearby doorway. "We saved it for you".

"Seriously?" I reply. It's weird, but even this simple gesture seems hugely important right now.

"Tuck in," Bob says with a smile.

I hurry over to the grill and slip the steak onto a plate, before grabbing a knife and fork and starting to eat. It's the best thing I've eaten for days; in fact, it might be the best thing I've eaten in my entire life. Juicy and filling, it feels like life itself. Even as I'm eating it, though, I can't help but worry about whether it'll be the last steak I ever eat. Putting the last piece into my mouth, I take a moment to savor the taste.

"Sorry if it's a little dry," Bob says

eventually. "We had to keep it cooking when we couldn't find you. Where'd you get to, anyway?"

"Just around," I reply, speaking with my mouth full.

"Good meat?" Bob asks.

"The best," I reply. "Thanks for sharing it".

"My pleasure," he says. "Feel free to lick your plate if you like. We're not standing on ceremony here. I figure we might as well eat it while it's still fresh. I've got a nice little stash from the convenience store, but I'm afraid we're gonna be eating mostly tinned food for a while. I just wanted to offer the steak as a kind of token of my appreciation for your efforts. You've both been very useful today, and I think we have a really good chance of making this work".

"Harrison Blake's gone," Henry says, staring at me.

"I figured," I reply.

"Fucking idiot," Bob adds. "The guy thinks he can just walk out of New York and find some new paradise on the other side of the fence. God knows what's got into his head, but I guess we're probably better off without him. People like that just end up slowing things down. I've seen his type before and they always end up causing trouble. He's just an idealist who doesn't realize how hard it is to do a proper job".

"Exactly," Henry says, sounding as if he's

desperate to agree with anything that Bob says. "He's an idealist". He spits that last word out, almost as if it's poison.

"It was really good food," I say, thankful for the meal, "but I'm tired. I think I might -"

"Should we show her?" Henry asks excitedly, turning to Bob.

"I don't know," Bob replies.

"Come on!" Henry continues. "You said we're in this together! She deserves the chance to see this, doesn't she? I know what you're thinking, but she'll prove you wrong". He turns to me. "You'll prove him wrong, won't you?"

"I have no idea," I reply. "What are you talking about?"

"Let's hold up a moment," Bob says. "Henry, do you really think your sister's ready for something like this? The last thing we need is to have her making problems. It might be better to keep some things behind closed doors".

"Show me what?" I ask, starting to get the feeling that there's some big joke that they're not sharing with me. I wait a moment, but they just seem to be enjoying my confusion. "Henry, what's going on?" I continue, turning to my brother. "What's this all about?"

"Okay," Bob says with a sigh, turning and walking through to the next room. "Come and see it. But I'm not gonna let you cause any trouble".

"What is it?" I ask Henry as soon as we're alone.

"Before we go through," he replies, "you need to understand something. Everything we do is for the good of the building as a whole. Bob's right. We have to look after ourselves, and that means treating outsiders as potential threats, at least until they've shown that we can trust them. We don't know how the world works right now, but we have to be careful".

I stare at him. "You sound more and more like Bob every time you open your mouth," I say eventually.

"Stop saying that," he replies. "Just accept that what you're about to see is totally necessary". He leads me over to the door. "I know what you're like, Elizabeth. You'll get funny about this at first, but once you think it through, you'll understand that it's the only way we can be sure that we're safe. When we meet someone new, we have to do this. It's not like the old days, when you knew you were safe from other people. Even the smallest mistake could be a total disaster".

"Someone new?" I ask.

"You'll see".

I follow him through to a room at the back of the building, where the last remaining sunlight is streaming in through a large window on the far side. "Henry," I say, starting to get really worried, "remind me to sit down and talk to you later about this hero worship thing you've got going on with Bob, okay? You're really starting to creep me out".

"There's no hero worship," Henry says. "I just recognize when someone understands the nature of the changing world dynamic. You'll see".

The nature of the changing world dynamic? Those words don't sound anything like something Henry would say. It's pretty obvious that his head's full of regurgitated ideas and phrases from Bob.

"Okay," Henry says as we walk through to yet another back room in this labyrinthine rear section of the building. "Get ready for it".

Finally, I spot Bob over in a far corner, and I see to my shock that he's got someone tied to a chair. At first, I assume it must be Harrison Blake, but as I get closer I see that it's actually a girl. In fact, it's the girl from earlier; it's the thin girl who came out of the pharmacy, and she's tied down with a series of thick ropes, while a white bandage is tied over her mouth to keep her from speaking. There's genuine fear in her eyes, and she stares at me as if she thinks she's about to be killed. I don't blame her: if I was tied up by a bunch of people I didn't know, in a place like this, I'd be scared for my life as well.

"What are -" I start to say, my heart racing.

"Now before you ask any questions," Bob says, interrupting me, "let me make one thing clear. It was not my idea to show you this, Elizabeth. I assumed that you'd be unable to grasp the realities of our situation, but your brother assures me that you're a little more mature. He told me to trust you, so I'm going to be completely honest here and tell you in no uncertain terms what we're dealing with. This is a very delicate situation, and it's something we need to handle with tact and grace".

"What are you doing to her?" I ask, turning to Henry. It's hard to believe that his adoration of Bob has reached the point where he's willing to be an accomplice to something like this.

"I believe we have a spy in our midst," Bob continues.

"A spy?" I turn back to him, stunned by the way he's talking. It's as if he thinks he's in the middle of some kind of war movie.

"Someone who came to acquire information about us," Bob adds, "and who is then going to feed that information back to others".

"No," I say, swallowing hard as the girl continues to stare wide-eyed at me. "No way. You can't be serious. Look at her, she's not a spy!"

"Yes way, I'm afraid," Bob says. "Now, as long as this nice young lady has nothing to hide, she'll be free within twenty-four hours. My concern, however, is that she's been sent to observe us and to gather information. Someone wants to know what we've got stored up here, and how many people we've got guarding our supplies. I don't know who's watching us, but we've attracted some serious attention, and I'm not gonna let anyone compromise the security of our stockpile. I will not be the first one to make an aggressive move, but I will certainly defend myself if I feel that I'm being threatened. That's just the kind of man I am".

"Where did you find her?" I ask.

"She was poking around in the street outside," he continues. "My reckoning is she must have followed us back here earlier. I kept an eye on her for a few minutes from one of the windows, and then she came into the foyer. She was being very quiet, very careful, like she didn't want anyone to know she was here. Just prowling around like she wanted to get the lie of the place. Fortunately, she didn't get very far".

"Bob's gonna make sure she's safe," Henry says. "It's a necessary evil".

"I'll be loosening the gag shortly," Bob explains.

"Let me save you the trouble," I say, stepping forward and reaching out to untie the girl.

"No!" Henry shouts, grabbing my arm and pulling me back. "Let Bob do this!" he says, holding me firmly. "This is a life or death situation. Don't embarrass me, Elizabeth!"

"Embarrass you?" I stare at him, finding it hard to believe that Bob's managed to indoctrinate him quite so successfully in such a short period of time. It's less than four full days since this situation started, and already my brother seems to have become part of some kind of armed group. "Are you serious?" I say after a moment. "Look at her! She's not dangerous. She's just like us. She's terrified. You can't tie people up when -"

"This is not a normal situation," Bob says, sounding like some kind of military textbook. I'm starting to think he's gone off the deep end, and that he's living in some kind of fantasy world in which he's the general in charge of a small army, facing a potential war. "We're effectively in a state of martial law," he continues. "Now, I'm going to suggest that all three of us interview this young lady and ascertain that she means us no harm. Seems to me, there's gonna be no trouble provided she's honest with us and provided she doesn't give us any cause for concern".

"Elizabeth!" Henry hisses. "You have to understand -"

"You have to untie her," I say. "You have to untie her right now!"

Bob stares at me for a moment, before wandering over and stopping right in front of me. "I fully understand why you might not like this situation," he says, "but some things just have to be done, whether any of us like them or not. I'm giving you the opportunity to prove yourself by participating in this process of discovery, but I assure you that you're totally at liberty to just go upstairs, go to sleep and pretend that none of this is happening. Just remember one thing. Anyone who's not fully committed to the cause is, effectively, a drain on our resources and that's not a situation that can be tolerated in the long-term. I'm going to keep this building and its occupants safe from outside threats, and I'm willing to use extreme measures in order to do so". He pauses for a moment, looking deep into my eyes as if he wants to see right into my soul. "So what's it gonna be, Elizabeth? Are you with us or are you against us?"

Turning to Henry, I see a look of total contempt on his face. It's as if he's seeing me through Bob's eyes, and agreeing with every word that comes from Bob's lips. For the first time, I start to realize that if Henry has to choose between the pair of us, he might not choose me.

*Continued in:*

Days 5 to 8
(Mass Extinction Event book 2)

*Also by Amy Cross*

**The Devil, the Witch and the Whore**
**(The Deal book 1)**

*"Leave the forest alone. Whatever's out there, just let it be. Don't make it angry."*

When a horrific discovery is made at the edge of town, Sheriff James Kopperud realizes the answers he seeks might be waiting beyond in the vast forest. But everybody in the town of Deal knows that there's something out there in the forest, something that should never be disturbed. A deal was made long ago, a deal that was supposed to keep the town safe. And if he insists on investigating the murder of a local girl, James is going to have to break that deal and head out into the wilderness.

Meanwhile, James has no idea that his estranged daughter Ramsey has returned to town. Ramsey is running from something, and she thinks she can find safety in the vast tunnel system that runs beneath the forest. Before long, however, Ramsey finds herself coming face to face with creatures that hide in the shadows. One of these creatures is known as the devil, and another is known as the witch. They're both waiting for the whore to arrive, but for very different reasons. And soon Ramsey is offered a terrible deal, one that could save or destroy the entire town, and maybe even the world.

*Also by Amy Cross*

**The Soul Auction**

"I saw a woman on the beach. I watched her face a demon."

Thirty years after her mother's death, Alice Ashcroft is drawn back to the coastal English town of Curridge. Somebody in Curridge has been reviewing Alice's novels online, and in those reviews there have been tantalizing hints at a hidden truth. A truth that seems to be linked to her dead mother.

"Thirty years ago, there was a soul auction."

Once she reaches Curridge, Alice finds strange things happening all around her. Something attacks her car. A figure watches her on the beach at night. And when she tries to find the person who has been reviewing her books, she makes a horrific discovery.

What really happened to Alice's mother thirty years ago? Who was she talking to, just moments before dropping dead on the beach? What caused a huge rockfall that nearly tore a nearby cliff-face in half? And what sinister presence is lurking in the grounds of the local church?

*Also by Amy Cross*

**Darper Danver: The Complete First Series**

Five years ago, three friends went to a remote cabin in the woods and tried to contact the spirit of a long-dead soldier. They thought they could control whatever happened next. They were wrong...

Newly released from prison, Cassie Briggs returns to Fort Powell, determined to get her life back on track. Soon, however, she begins to suspect that an ancient evil still lurks in the nearby cabin. Was the mysterious Darper Danver really destroyed all those years ago, or does her spirit still linger, waiting for a chance to return?

As Cassie and her ex-boyfriend Fisher are finally forced to face the truth about what happened in the cabin, they realize that Darper isn't ready to let go of their lives just yet. Meanwhile, a vengeful woman plots revenge for her brother's murder, and a New York ghost writer arrives in town to uncover the truth. Before long, strange carvings begin to appear around town and blood starts to flow once again.

*Also by Amy Cross*

**The Ghost of Molly Holt**

"Molly Holt is dead. There's nothing to fear in this house."

When three teenagers set out to explore an abandoned house in the middle of a forest, they think they've found the location where the infamous Molly Holt video was filmed.

They've found much more than that...

Tim doesn't believe in ghosts, but he has a crush on a girl who does. That's why he ends up taking her out to the house, and it's also why he lets her take his only flashlight. But as they explore the house together, Tim and Becky start to realize that something else might be lurking in the shadows.

Something that, ten years ago, suffered unimaginable pain.

Something that won't rest until a terrible wrong has been put right.

*Also by Amy Cross*

**American Coven**

He kidnapped three women and held them in his basement. He thought they couldn't fight back. He was wrong...

Snatched from the street near her home, Holly Carter is taken to a rural house and thrown down into a stone basement. She meets two other women who have also been kidnapped, and soon Holly learns about the horrific rituals that take place in the house. Eventually, she's called upstairs to take her place in the ice bath.

As her nightmare continues, however, Holly learns about a mysterious power that exists in the basement, and which the three women might be able to harness. When they finally manage to get through the metal door, however, the women have no idea that their fight for freedom is going to stretch out for more than a decade, or that it will culminate in a final, devastating demonstration of their new-found powers.

*Also by Amy Cross*

**The Ash House**

Why would anyone ever return to a haunted house?

For Diane Mercer the answer is simple. She's dying of cancer, and she wants to know once and for all whether ghosts are real.

Heading home with her young son, Diane is determined to find out whether the stories are real. After all, everyone else claimed to see and hear strange things in the house over the years. Everyone except Diane had some kind of experience in the house, or in the little ash house in the yard.

As Diane explores the house where she grew up, however, her son is exploring the yard and the forest. And while his mother might be struggling to come to terms with her own impending death, Daniel Mercer is puzzled by fleeting appearances of a strange little girl who seems drawn to the ash house, and by strange, rasping coughs that he keeps hearing at night.

*The Ash House* is a horror novel about a woman who desperately wants to know what will happen to her when she dies, and about a boy who uncovers the shocking truth about a young girl's murder.

*Also by Amy Cross*

**Haunted**

Twenty years ago, the ghost of a dead little girl drove Sheriff Michael Blaine to his death.

Now, that same ghost is coming for his daughter.

Returning to the small town where she grew up, Alex Roberts is determined to live a normal, quiet life. For the residents of Railham, however, she's an unwelcome reminder of the town's darkest hour.

Twenty years ago, nine-year-old Mo Garvey was found brutally murdered in a nearby forest. Everyone thinks that Alex's father was responsible, but if the killer was brought to justice, why is the ghost of Mo Garvey still after revenge?

And how far will the real killer go to protect his secret, when Alex starts getting closer to the truth?

*Haunted* is a horror novel about a woman who has to face her past, about a town that would rather forget, and about a little girl who refuses to let death stand in her way.

*Also by Amy Cross*

**The Curse of Wetherley House**

"If you walk through that door, Evil Mary will get you."

When she agrees to visit a supposedly haunted house with an old friend, Rosie assumes she'll encounter nothing more scary than a few creaks and bumps in the night. Even the legend of Evil Mary doesn't put her off. After all, she knows ghosts aren't real. But when Mary makes her first appearance, Rosie realizes she might already be trapped.

For more than a century, Wetherley House has been cursed. A horrific encounter on a remote road in the late 1800's has already caused a chain of misery and pain for all those who live at the house. Wetherley House was abandoned long ago, after a terrible discovery in the basement, something has remained undetected within its room. And even the local children know that Evil Mary waits in the house for anyone foolish enough to walk through the front door.

Before long, Rosie realizes that her entire life has been defined by the spirit of a woman who died in agony. Can she become the first person to escape Evil Mary, or will she fall victim to the same fate as the house's other occupants?

*Also by Amy Cross*

**The Ghosts of Hexley Airport**

Ten years ago, more than two hundred people died in a horrific plane crash at Hexley Airport.

Today, some say their ghosts still haunt the terminal building.

When she starts her new job at the airport, working a night shift as part of the security team, Casey assumes the stories about the place can't be true. Even when she has a strange encounter in a deserted part of the departure hall, she's certain that ghosts aren't real.

Soon, however, she's forced to face the truth. Not only is there something haunting the airport's buildings and tarmac, but a sinister force is working behind the scenes to replicate the circumstances of the original accident. And as a snowstorm moves in, Hexley Airport looks set to witness yet another disaster.

*Also by Amy Cross*

**The Girl Who Never Came Back**

Twenty years ago, Charlotte Abernathy vanished while playing near her family's house. Despite a frantic search, no trace of her was found until a year later, when the little girl turned up on the doorstep with no memory of where she'd been.

Today, Charlotte has put her mysterious ordeal behind her, even though she's never learned where she was during that missing year. However, when her eight-year-old niece vanishes in similar circumstances, a fully-grown Charlotte is forced to make a fresh attempt to uncover the truth.

Originally published in 2013, the fully revised and updated version of *The Girl Who Never Came Back* tells the harrowing story of a woman who thought she could forget her past, and of a little girl caught in the tangled web of a dark family secret.

*Also by Amy Cross*

**Asylum**
**(The Asylum Trilogy book 1)**

"No-one ever leaves Lakehurst. The staff, the patients, the ghosts... Once you're here, you're stuck forever."

After shooting her little brother dead, Annie Radford is sent to Lakehurst psychiatric hospital for assessment. Hearing voices in her head, Annie is forced to undergo experimental new treatments devised by a mysterious old man who lives in the hospital's attic. It soon becomes clear that the hospital's staff, led by the vicious Nurse Winter, are hiding something horrific at Lakehurst.

As Annie struggles to survive the hospital, she learns more about Nurse Winter's own story. Once a promising young medical student, Kirsten Winter also heard voices in her head. Voices that traveled a long way to reach her. Voices that have a plan of their own. Voices that will stop at nothing to get what they want.

What kind of signals are being transmitted from the basement of the hospital? Who is the old man in the attic? Why are living human brains kept in jars? And what is the dark secret that lurks at the heart of the hospital?

*Also by Amy Cross*

**The Devil's Hand**

"I felt it last night! I was all alone, and suddenly a hand touched my shoulder!"

The year is 1943. Beacon's Ash is a private, remote school in the North of England, and all its pupils are fallen girls. Pregnant and unmarried, they have been sent away by their families. For Ivy Jones, a young girl who arrived at the school several months earlier, Beacon's Ash is a nightmare, and her fears are strengthened when one of her classmates is killed in mysterious circumstances.

Has the ghost of Abigail Cartwright returned to the school? Who or what is responsible for the hand that touches the girls' shoulders in the dead of night? And is the school's headmaster Jeremiah Kane just a madman who seeks to cause misery, or is he in fact on the trail of the Devil himself? Soon ghosts are stalking the dark corridors, and Ivy realizes she has to face the evil that lurks in the school's shadows.

*The Devil's Hand* is a horror novel about a girl who seeks the truth about her friend's death, and about a madman who believes the Devil stalks the school's corridors in the run-up to Christmas.

For more information, visit:

www. amycross.com

Made in the USA
San Bernardino, CA
27 February 2019